# *The* FINAL EXEMPLAR *of* ELIZABETH ANN

# The FINAL EXEMPLAR of ELIZABETH ANN

*Volume Three: The Elizabeth Ann Trilogy*

J. NICHOLS MOWERY

THE FINAL EXEMPLAR OF ELIZABETH ANN
Volume Three: The Elizabeth Ann Trilogy

Copyright © 2017 J. Nichols Mowery.

All rights reserved. No part of this book may be used or reproduced by any means, graphic, electronic, or mechanical, including photocopying, recording, taping or by any information storage retrieval system without the written permission of the author except in the case of brief quotations embodied in critical articles and reviews.

This is a work of fiction. All of the characters, names, incidents, organizations, and dialogue in this novel are either the products of the author's imagination or are used fictitiously.

iUniverse books may be ordered through booksellers or by contacting:

iUniverse
1663 Liberty Drive
Bloomington, IN 47403
www.iuniverse.com
1-800-Authors (1-800-288-4677)

Because of the dynamic nature of the Internet, any web addresses or links contained in this book may have changed since publication and may no longer be valid. The views expressed in this work are solely those of the author and do not necessarily reflect the views of the publisher, and the publisher hereby disclaims any responsibility for them.

Any people depicted in stock imagery provided by Thinkstock are models, and such images are being used for illustrative purposes only. Certain stock imagery © Thinkstock.

ISBN: 978-1-5320-1873-2 (sc)
ISBN: 978-1-5320-1874-9 (e)

Library of Congress Control Number: 2017905885

Print information available on the last page.

iUniverse rev. date: 05/10/2017

# CONTENTS

*Prologue* . . . . . . . . . . . . . . . . . . . . . . . . . . . . . . . . . . . . . . . . . . . . . . .vii

Chapter 1     June 1st—Liz. . . . . . . . . . . . . . . . . . . . . . . . . . . . . . . . . 1
Chapter 2     June 1st—Beth . . . . . . . . . . . . . . . . . . . . . . . . . . . . . . . 19
Chapter 3     June 1st—Ann. . . . . . . . . . . . . . . . . . . . . . . . . . . . . . . . 30
Chapter 4     June 5th—Liz . . . . . . . . . . . . . . . . . . . . . . . . . . . . . . . . 39
Chapter 5     June 5th—Beth . . . . . . . . . . . . . . . . . . . . . . . . . . . . . . . 60
Chapter 6     June 5th—Ann . . . . . . . . . . . . . . . . . . . . . . . . . . . . . . . 76
Chapter 7     June 10th—Liz . . . . . . . . . . . . . . . . . . . . . . . . . . . . . . . 95
Chapter 8     June 10th—Beth . . . . . . . . . . . . . . . . . . . . . . . . . . . . . 106
Chapter 9     June 10th—Ann . . . . . . . . . . . . . . . . . . . . . . . . . . . . . 117
Chapter 10    June 15th—Together. . . . . . . . . . . . . . . . . . . . . . . . . . 126
Chapter 11    June 15th—Liz . . . . . . . . . . . . . . . . . . . . . . . . . . . . . . 136
Chapter 12    June 15th—Beth . . . . . . . . . . . . . . . . . . . . . . . . . . . . . 146
Chapter 13    June 15th—Ann . . . . . . . . . . . . . . . . . . . . . . . . . . . . . 152
Chapter 14    June 20th—The Summer Solstice Liz. . . . . . . . . . . . . . 160
Chapter 15    June 20th—The Summer Solstice Beth. . . . . . . . . . . . . 167
Chapter 16    June 20th—The Summer Solstice Ann . . . . . . . . . . . . . 172

# PROLOGUE

Two years ago, on the first day of June, life changing tragedies sent each Parallel Life of Elizabeth Ann Anderson into a tailspin. The energy force from each of these events recoiled within the Universe causing each like-kind dimension to mesh together at certain focal points. The dimensions for the Parallel Lives of Elizabeth Ann came together at the focused point of the large glowing golden agate set into the floor of the cabin built by James Anderson for his family: his wife, Jill and his two daughters, toddler Dana Marie and infant Elizabeth Ann.

During that month of June, Liz Day, Beth Anderson and Eliza Staples encountered each other within the space of their own homes. Each became aware that these other women were the exact physical being as she was. With each of these encounters, the three Elizabeth Anns became aware of the remarkable likeness of the other two to herself and that they each claimed the cabin as their own place was undeniable. After many astonishing encounters, the women eventually came to understand that they were Parallel Lives from an original child named Elizabeth Ann Anderson.

They also came to understand that each existed in a separate dimensional plain and lived an entirely different and separate life. Their only connection to the other dimensions was at the golden stone which their father James Anderson set into the cement floor when building his cabin at Redcliff's Beach.

In that month of June, the three Elizabeth Ann Andersons came face to face with the consequences of their life path choices and the events forced upon them by the Universes energy. By the time the Summer Solstice came around, these three Parallel Lives of Elizabeth Ann understood that their own life choices also impacted the other Elizabeth Anns lives.

The following year, when the month of June came around, the three women fully a part of each other's life and met daily at the adjoined tables over the golden stone in the floor of their cabins. At these times, they shared the events and discoveries within their own lives.

All three tell of experiences in new dimensions, both frightening and wondrous. It is when they each find a cave filled with crystal formations and fire-opal tiles on the floor that they realize there is more meaning at their meeting each other than some accident from space. Other dimensions take through rapidly changing zones to encounter unknown Parallel Lives. They see dimensions from eons in the past, then go into dimensions eons into the future. In many of these dimensions they encounter unknown Elizabeth Anns who never see them and which they never get to know.

The weeks before their second Summer Solstice, the three Elizabeth Anns of Redcliff's Beach experience unknown dimensions or have their dimension switch to the others. During those days, two Parallel Live lose one of their own as another Parallel Life of Elizabeth comes into their lives.

During that month of June, each Parallel Life of Elizabeth Ann becomes aware that the animals which are part of their lives are their animal-familiars. Animals who came to lead them safely through the amazing experiences they each encounter.

It is during the Summer Solstice near the end of that June, that each of the Elizabeth Ann Andersons accept what the touchstone has told them, that Beth Anderson is the original child named Elizabeth Ann Anderson.

# ONE

*June 1ˢᵗ—Liz*

LIZ slaps the golden stone in the north cliff face of Redcliff's Beach and shouts, "I declare this run good and done." When nothing happens to send her into another dimensions, she is surprised and turns to face down the beach. Its then that something pushes against her left leg and she looks down at Kip, her amazing Norwegian elkhound dog. "Hey Kip. Looks like we're to stay where we are today. What do you think of that?"

*It's okay. We need to get home. Someone is too close to our house. Are you expecting anyone?*

"Who is it? Can you tell if it's a man or woman? I expect the other to come to the adjoined tables this noon. Is the person inside or outside of the house?"

In answer, Kip barks three times and leaps off the edge of the granite slab. Following him south along the wet packed sand left by the last high tide, Liz races after him. Trotting ahead of her, Kip slows every so often to let Liz catch up to him. Only when they reach the flag pole at the entrance of the path, through the dunes, to her home, does the dog stop to wait. When Liz gets to him, Kip gives her a wrinkle nosed grin.

Laughing at his silly look, Liz grabs hold of his thick coat and gives him a loving rubdown, saying, "This run is way too easy for you, my ageless one. I admit I'm slower now that I'm in the over fifty club. Thanks for staying close and not winning by the wide distance you really could."

Again, the dog grins up at her as his words fill her head,

*We're not home yet. Last one there is a rotten egg.*

Without waiting, Liz turns up the path and runs hard trying to reach the deck, a hundred feet further away. Again, Kip passes her at a steady trot and a few feet away from the steps up to the deck, takes one last bounding leap. When he lands next to the bottom step, he yipes loudly, stumbles and crashes onto the railing and bottom step. Immediately, the animal stands and turns to Liz and she sees he uses only three of his legs and is holding his right leg high to lick at the blood dripping from that paw.

When she reaches the dog, Liz gently lifts the injured leg and looks at the bottom of the paw. At that time, she sees is a thick shard of glass poking out from between two of the pads on the foot. Trying to remove the glass only makes the blood flow faster, so Liz pulls off her headscarf and gently wraps it around Kip's foot. When he whines pathetically and she sees how much blood is dripping from the wound, Liz picks Kip up in her arms and helps him to the slider door off the deck.

Taking the animal directly through the cabin, she gets to the rug in front of the door out to the garage and tells him, "Wait here. I need to run up and get my purse and keys. Don't move."

For those moments, Kip sits on the door's entry rug and licks at the soggy scarf. A minute later, Liz is back, opens the door and again lifts him onto his back feet so they can move into the garage. Once she has Kip on the front passenger seat of her car, she tosses her purse on the back seat, gets behind the steering wheel and asks, "Are you in much pain?"

*Not bad, but I'm losing a lot of blood.*

"Yes, I can see that. I've heard Dan Parker's new partner in his veterinary office is a woman and very good. We'll go see her. I'm sorry to say this, Kip, but I'd only let Dan work on your wound as a last resort."

The animal lays his chin on her right leg and closes his eyes,

*It's a bad cut. More glass is inside. I'll need deep stitches.*

Driving with speeds too fast for Shoreline Drive, Liz thinks only of getting Kip the help he needs. When she reaches the turnoff into Ocean Shores, she gently touches him and asks, "Are you still with me, my dear friend?"

Looking up at her, the dogs says,

*I'm here but have lost much blood. Sorry about the seat cover. Know that I love you, dear one, I always will.*

"I love you, too, darling Kip. We'll be there in a minute."

The next few minutes are the longest minutes Liz has ever spent and she silently gives thanks that there are no patrolmen waiting with their usual radar traps. Then she zips down the main street, through a red light and turns into the parking lot in front of Parker's office building directly across the street from the IGA grocery store she always shops for groceries.

Seconds later, she has parked in a handicap space only a few feet from the front door of the veterinarian's office. Jumping out of the car, Liz races into the office, and shouts, "I need help. My dog is seriously hurt and bleeding to death."

The wide eyed receptionist points to a gurney beside her desk and yells, "Take and get him out of your car. I'll get some help."

Taking hold of the gurney's handle. Liz moves the rolling bed out the automatic door and to the passenger side door of her car. Opening the door as wide as possible, she watches Kip struggling to sit up by himself. Instantly, she reaches in and lifts the large dog out onto the bed of the gurney. At that time, the bloody scarf drops from his paw to the pavement beside the car. Ignoring it, Liz places the dog on the cart and turns towards the office door where she sees it is held open by a tall dark haired woman dressed in surgical blues.

Liz shouts, "This is Kip. He stepped on sharp glass and is bleeding profusely. I couldn't remove the large piece of glass in his paw and he says there's more."

Without comment, the woman pulls the gurney in through the

entry doors and introduces herself over her shoulder, "I'm Dr. Irene Vale, Dr. Parker's new partner. Go open the furthest door at the end of the waiting room. It goes directly to my surgery."

Liz rushes to where the doctor points, opens the door wide and helps the woman guide the gurney up to the surgical table. As the doctor checks the cut paw, Liz watches silently. Immediately, Dr. Vale says, "Help me lift him onto the surgery table. Don't mind the blood. He's fairly alert and bright eyed."

Without answering, Liz gently lifts Kip's rear end onto the operating table as the doctor lifts his front end and watches as the woman positions the right leg until it extends straight out. At that time, a young woman, also dressed in surgical clothes, enters the room and begins to wash the wound with a bottle of liquid. It's then that the doctor says to Liz, "Get out of here. Go sit in the waiting room. This is my assistant, Kerstin. She'll help with the surgery. You'd be in the way. Close the door after you. Kip's in good hands. I promise he'll be fine."

Leaving the room, Liz closes the door and goes back through the office and out to the still open car door. Grabbing her purse from the back seat, she makes certain the doors are closed and locked. Then, leaving the car parked where it was, Liz goes back into the waiting room and sits on a small sofa close to the door where she'd left Kip.

Now that Kip's fate is out of her hands, the reality of the last thirty minutes hits Liz and she begins to cry softly. After a few minutes, Liz feels a soft tap on her left shoulder and she looks up to see Dr. Dan Parker standing a few feet in front of her. In his right hand he is holding a box of tissues out to her. "Here, Liz, take these. You're looking pretty damp. Has something happened to Kip?"

Taking the box from him, Liz pulls several tissues from it, wipes her face and blows her nose loudly before looking at the man who'd so rudely dumped her nearly a year ago. When she does, all she says is, "Thanks, I needed that," Then she pulls out several more tissues and hands the box back to him.

When she doesn't say anything more, Parker repeats, "Can you tell me what happened to Kip?"

Squinting up at the man, Liz answers, "He stepped on broken glass hidden in the sand next to the steps up to the deck. Luckily it wasn't far from the house and I was able to get him out to the car. He lost a lot of blood. Your new vet, Dr. Vale, and her assistant are working on him now. She seems very competent. I would guess her qualifications are excellent or you wouldn't have brought her into your office."

As she speaks to Parker, it suddenly hits her that she feels absolutely nothing for this person, this man, this Dr. Dan Parker who talked of love, melted her heart and then broke it into a thousand pieces. It is these thoughts, zipping through Liz's head that stop her from responding to Dan Parker any further.

Staring at the door where she knows Kip is being treated by Dr. Vale, Liz slowly becomes aware that Dan is still standing next to her holding the box of tissues. Letting the silence continue, it is several minutes before Parker asks, "How have things been going for you before this happened?"

Squinting up at him against the bright office lighting, Liz looks at him with a puzzled look and says, "Really, Dan, I have nothing more to say to you. Thanks for the tissues. Right now, I need to use that restroom across the room. Excuse me."

Without another word, she walks across the reception room and goes in through the door marked with a gilded 'W'. When she comes out the door, a few minutes later, Liz looks refreshed as she walks back to the same sofa she'd left and sits down. Seeing no sign of Parker, she sighs with relief and picks up a new looking magazine off the end table beside her. Thumbing through it, one of the articles catches her eye and she reads the title, "Who chooses whom, pet or person?"

Intrigued, Liz sees the article is formed around the author's beliefs and observations as a former Marine and retired veterinarian. As she reads, she is pleased the article enforces her own belief that Kip chose her. To back his theory, the author suggests that the connection is as much mental and it is physical or through contact or smell. Then he tells stories of several pet owners who had felt a connection the moment they saw the animals they would chose. These animals lived many years with their owners and became more friends than just pets. It seems that the owner felt able to handle life altering changes with positive attitudes.

When she gets to the end of the article, Liz tears out the man's name and email information from the end of the article. "Rudy Sloan, DVM, PhD and LOA. Now retired from his practice in Seattle, Washington." Liz reads softly to herself then tucks the slip of paper into her purse and lays the magazine back on the end table. Just then, Dr. Vale opens the door of her surgery and walks over to where Liz sits.

"Kip is doing fine. We had to give him a unit of serum to counter the loss of so much blood. Even so, he seems quite alert. If you feel comfortable about doing so, you may take him home today. Just watch over him the next few days, I think this would be best for both of you. Change his bandage daily and give him the medication I'll send home with him. Make certain he eats some food and drinks at least a quart of water before you tuck him down for the night. Kip was correct, there was another piece of the glass deeper in his pad. That's what nicked a vein and caused the loss of so much blood.

"I've given him a round of antibiotics as his record has him getting the full regime of shots only a year ago. I don't think he'll suffer with the wound. It was clean from all the bloodletting and should heal quickly. Leave the bandage on tonight then put fresh ones around noon and for three days. If he chews at his paw, put this collar on him. Do you feel comfortable about taking care of him?"

"Oh, yes. Kip's very good about doing what I ask of him. I'll make certain he understands the bandages must stay on until we see you again. Would three days be a good time to bring him back? Good. Can I go see him now?"

"Of course, He's still pretty groggy and will be for the next few hours. Kristine is with him as he's still on the operating table. It'll be a lot easier getting him into the car from the gurney. Come on, take a good look at him, then I'll help you get him settled in your car."

Standing, Liz nods, then follows the doctor into the surgery. There she sees a groggy Kip lying on his side on a table with a thick rubber pad under him. Putting both hands on his head, Kip opens his eyes and looks up at her,

*Hello, dear one, can we go home now?*

Smiling at him, Liz says, "Yes. We'll go as soon as the good doctor finishes your paperwork. How do you feel? Dr. Vale said you're going to be fine if you follow her instructions. She gave you a unit of serum to make you strong and wrapped your foot with a lovely bandage that must stay untouched for a day and night. I'll change it for clean ones the next three days. When we get home, I'll bring your bed downstairs put it near the golden stone for you. While you are there, I'll sleep on the sofa and camp downstairs for a week. Dr. Vale wants you back here in three days to see how you've healed. You must leave the wound alone or you'll have to wear the collar of shame. Do you understand?"

Kip looks into eyes and says,

*Yes, dear one. Dr. Vale did a great job. I'll be good at home.*

Kissing the side of his head, Liz smooths his coat as she stares at the thick bandage on his right paw. Then she says, "I love you, darling friend. Do you want to sit up?"

When he does, Liz looks at Dr. Vale and says, "He seems very ready to go home. I'll tuck him on his bed and call in the morning to let you know how he is."

*Good. Now let's go home.*

Still turned toward the doctor, Liz says, "Thank you for taking care of him so quickly. It looked like a very nasty cut. Could I get the piece of glass you found in him? I'm going to try to find where it was and what it came from. I'll let you know what I find."

The veterinarian reaches into a large sink, nearby, rinses off an ugly piece of clear glass and wraps it in a paper towel. Handing the wad to Liz, Dr. Vale says, "It looks as if it came from of a liquor bottle or something like it. It definitely hadn't washed in on the waves. Edges of sea glass are rounded edges and wouldn't cut anything. This piece is one mean looking fragment of glass."

Liz frowns as she takes the object and says, "I didn't see any bottle or glass on top of the sand where we ran, so it must have been buried next to the steps up to my deck. Maybe the wind finally exposed it. I'll let you know if I find anything else. What time should I call tomorrow to let you know how Kip is doing?"

"Just after nine. However, if he gets a temperature, bring him back in here. I'll want to see him immediately. Understand?"

"Of course. I'll talk to you in the morning."

As the women talk, Kip sighs loudly and lays back down on the gurney, saying,

*I want to go home.*

Hearing him, Liz takes the papers from the Doctor and shakes her hand, thanking her again. Then she asks Kip, "Are you ready to ride out to the car or do you want to walk?"

*I would ride.*

Pulling the gurney out through the office's sliding entry door, Liz steers the cart to the passenger side of the car. Dr. Vale guides it from behind and pushes it up to the passenger side door. Its then that Kip tells her,

*Thank Dr. Vale for me. She's a very good doctor.*

Turning the vet, Liz says, "Kip wants me to thank you and tell you he thinks you're a very good doctor."

Looking at the dog, the veterinarian laughs. "Well I think he is one of the best animals I've ever had the pleasure to stitch up. You two take care of each other."

Once Kip is settled on the car seat, he suddenly growls loudly. At the same time, Liz sees a person is putting a slip of paper under the left windshield wiper. Pulling her head out from inside, Liz shouts, "Hey you, there, take that paper out of there.... Oh my-gosh, you're a police officer. Is that a ticket you're leaving?"

"Yes, ma'am, you've been parked in a handicap zone for more than two hours."

"I know I don't have the necessary tabs to park here, but my dog, Kip, was very badly injured. Dr. Vale just did surgery on him. Could you please give me a warning instead of a fine? I've never used handicapped zones before this time, not ever."

The woman squints at Liz for several seconds then nods, takes the paper from under the wiper blade and hands it to Liz, saying "It's a warning ticket. Dr. Parker came out earlier and told me about your dog. Are you leaving now?"

"Yes, I get to take Kip home. Thanks for being so understanding."

"You can always park in this spot for up to an hour to load or unload an injured animal. Then you must move the car to another spot. Do you understand?"

Nodding, Liz smiles at the woman as she takes the ticket from the woman. Settling behind the steering wheel, she buckles the seatbelt around her and puts the car in reverse. In the rearview mirror, she can see the officer watching her from a patrol car, so Liz eases the car carefully onto Main Street. As she turns towards the four-way stop, Kip lays his head on her leg and heaves a long sigh and Liz says, "Go to sleep, darling Kip. I love you. We'll be home soon."

Late in the afternoon, her kitchen phone rings and Liz answers with, "Hello, this is Liz." Instead of hearing a response, she hears only sounds of heavy breathing and panting. Quickly holding the phone away from her face, she puts two fingers between her lips and blows a long shrill whistle into the phone's mouth piece. Chuckling, she puts the receiver back onto the phone's cradle and wonders which kid from the local school just lost hearing in one ear.

Then she sees Kip is sitting up next to the stone under the dining table and staring at her.

*What was that for? Do you need help? Is someone here?*

Smiling, Liz says, "Sorry, dear friend. There was a moaner-groaner on the other end of the phone. I whistled loudly to teach him a lesson. I doubt he'll call anyone for a while. How are you feeling, my friend?"

*It is so good to be home. Could you check to see if my cut is healed?*

Kneeling beside the long table, Liz carefully takes Kip's paw and unwraps the thick bandage. When his pad is exposed, she nods, "Looks as if the golden agate is doing its magic again. Your cut is only a bright pink line. However, stay next to the stone the rest of the afternoon. Does it hurt at all? No? Good. How about when I touch the sides? That's so good. Still, stay on the stone a few hours longer. I'm going out to look for what cut you. I'll leave the door open in case you need to go potty. Don't go down to the sand. If you need to relieve yourself, do it on the side deck. I'll clean it up later. I repeat, do not go down to the sand."

Taking the long handled rake with her, Liz goes slowly down the steps to the beach path. Stopping beside the spot where Kip yelped, she works the rake through the soft dry sand. When she finds nothing after a few minutes, she thinks back to the last moments and remembers that Kip was leaping towards the steps not running. Turning around, she walks away from the steps and begins to reach out with the long handle and pulls the rake back through the sand.

Almost immediately, there is a soft clank as the metal tool hits and catches something in the sand. Slowly working the rake back towards her, Liz stops when half a broken whiskey bottle pops out of the sand. Surprised by what she sees, Liz exclaims, "My God, it's the bottom half of a broken whiskey bottle. How the hell did that get there? It looks new. Where the hell is the top part?"

Carefully picking up the broken bottle, she shakes loose sand from it and sees that a good amount of wet sand stays is on the bottom of the bottle. Lifting it to her nose, Liz sniffs at the jagged edge and the sharp odor of aged liquor causes her to cough. Quickly blowing air out her nostrils, she tries to clear the strong odor from her head.

Holding the bottle at arm's length, she sets it in the middle of the path and places the rake back near the mound of sand she just made. Slowly working the rake back and forth, Liz moves towards the steps to the deck. Again, there is the sharp clank of metal hitting glass and, when she pulls on the rake, the top half of a broken bottle appears. This bottle part has a dark smear of wet sand stuck along the sharp edge. Placing this bottle parts next to each other, Liz sees that, except for the piece which stuck in Kip's paw, the two broken bottle parts fit together to make one bottle.

"My God, it's no wonder Kip's foot was cut so deeply. It's a wonder I didn't step on it, considering where it was buried. I'm so glad it didn't cut his foot worse than it did. I'll tell Dr. Vale when I call her in the morning. That smell of liqueur is strong enough to make my eyes water, so it had to have been placed there recently. No more than a day or two. Couldn't be longer. That sand would have dried the liquid. It hasn't rained for over a week.

"Who would do that sort of thing and why would anyone want to hurt Kip? No. That wasn't for Kip. That bottle was placed there for anyone who uses the path. Someone who steps down hard as she's running. Someone like me... I'll be damned."

Dropping the rake along the path where she found the bottle, Liz carefully carries the two pieces of broken bottle up to the table on the deck. Then she quickly returns to where she left the rake and moves the sand around to see if there are any more hidden booby-traps. When she is certain there is nothing more, Liz returns to the deck and stares at the bottles on the deck table trying to decide what she should do with them.

*It seems someone is holding a grudge at something you or I have done.*

Looking over to the side of the deck, Liz sees Kip is lying on one of the chaise lounges and says, "Can you tell anything about the person who held this bottle besides me? I'm sure it was purposefully buried where it would do the most damage to someone. Whoever placed it there did so recently. Was it someone we know?"

*Yes, I smell the essence of Dan Parker. Remember how he turned away from us and left without a word last year? He is a religious zealot and believes what you told about us proved to him that we are evil creatures. I believe he wants us gone from this place. It seems he is making another move towards us and you must be very careful. I will keep a sharp watch for him.*

"That son of a bitch. Why would he do such a mean thing? We haven't spoken for over a year until today. Damn him." Liz sits on the edge of the lounge Kip is lying upon and rubs her hand over the dog's large head and says, "By the way, my friend, didn't I tell you to stay on the golden stone for another hour."

*I am fine and wanted to watch you find the broken glass. I was sure you would. Thank you.*

"Well, now that you're up, I'll fix lunch. Yours first, my dear friend. The good doctor said for you are to eat a good meal and to drink lots of water. Can you get off the lounge? Here, let me help you."

Once he's down on the deck, Kip follows Liz back inside and lays down beside the golden stone under the dining table. As he lowers his head onto its glowing surface, he heaves a loud sigh and Liz smiles at his dramatics as she goes into the kitchen. After filling his food dish with a mixture of hamburger meat and kibble, she places it near the end of the table and puts his water dish next to it. Only then does Kip look up and tell her,

*Many thanks, dear one. I'm more tired than I thought. Still, I'm hungry enough to eat a bear.*

Chuckling at his use of the old saying, Liz watches him eat from the dishes. When he has finished, the dog slowly stands and moves towards the door to the deck and she hears,

*Liz dear, I need to relieve myself. Would you open the door for me? I won't go into the sand.*

As she lets Kip onto the deck, Liz says, "I'm going to up to take a shower. When you come back in, lay on the golden stone again. We've got to make certain that wound is healed. It was a deep one."

When Liz returns, she has changed from her running shorts into a crisp cotton summer dress and goes into the kitchen. There, she pulls a large bowl from the fridge and sets it into a carry-all bag.

Sniffing the air, Kip says,

*That smells very good. Are we going somewhere?*

"Not we, only me this time. You stay home and rest. Tonight is the Jackson's neighborhood barbeque. I'm going over early to help Mary. She's always a bit puzzled about things like laying out plates and utensils. The bowl is potato salad. I made yesterday as I think it tastes better if it sets a day. If you really want to come, I'll take you and your bed in the car and drive over."

*No, I'll stay home. There'll be too many people who'll want to pet and poke at me. I'll stay and hold off any intruders. Okay?*

"More than okay. You defend the fort, general. I must say, it's good to hear your sense of humor is back. You really must be getting well." Liz tells the dog as she kisses his forehead before she starts towards the front door. Halfway there, the kitchen phone rings and she says, "Whoever it is can leave a message."

After four rings, voicemail picks up and a message is left. As she reaches for the handle on the front door, the phone rings again and she decides it may be one of the Jacksons needing her to bring something for them, so Liz answers it. Before the receiver gets to her left ear, a shrill whistle comes from earpiece. After that, a deep voice hisses, "Take that, you damned bitch."

Dropping the receiver onto the phone's cradle, Liz frowns and says, "This morning's prankster is trying to even the score. I'm turning off this house phone for a few days and lock the house up before I leave so you'll be safe, dear one. Sleep and get well. I'm off to rescue Mary."

Hurrying up the driveway to path through across the four wooded acres between her home and the Jacksons' house, Liz remembers when Alex Petrow lived in the house where they do now. The memory brings an overwhelming wave of sadness over Liz and she stops next to a twisted shore pine. Leaning against the ancient tree trunk, she thinks of the once good friend who tried to kill and was instead killed by others sent to protect Liz.

Exiting the thick stand of shore pines and manzanita brush at the edge of her acreage, Liz walks towards the Jackson's house where Larry Jackson is working over a large silver grill set on the side deck. When she gets closer, Liz sees he is standing watch over a large smoking hunk of sputtering meat that is slowly turning on the grill's spit. Knowing to announce her arrival before she starts up the steps, Liz shouts, "Whatever you're cooking on the spit smells delicious, Larry. I can hardly wait."

Larry turns to greet her and waves a soggy basting mop her way and says, "I hope it's as good as it smells, Liz. I sure don't want the damn thing to end up like the piece of leather I did last year."

Laughing at his self-imposed frenzy, Liz goes on through the open French doors at the back of the house. Inside, Mary is working at the kitchen counter and greets her friend as Liz sets the carryall bag on the counter. Both then turn to the other and give quick hugs. Mary beams at Liz and says, "You and you're potato salad are more than welcome. In fact, you're in time to do the tables. As usual, I'm running late. Take those trays with the utensils and napkins out to the buffet table. There's a pile of table coverings on this end of the first table. I'll bring the plates. I'm afraid Larry is still wrestling with that hunk of meat and I'm praying it won't end up like that piece of charcoal he created last year.

"Honestly, Liz, I've never understood why everyone thinks they have to grill outside when we all have wonderful temperature controlled ovens. Guess it's a holdover of Neanderthal DNA in the male species. Do you think all that smoke really makes the meat taste better? Yeah? Well not me. Know this, my dear friend, if you ever hear me say I love barbeque, slap me hard."

Laughing, Liz takes the trays indicated out to the deck and sets them on a bench. As she covers the tables, Mary comes outside with a basket of dishes and glassware. Working quickly, Liz sets the napkin wrapped eating utensils as Mary places the plates and glasses. Neither says a word to the other as they go about laying out the tables, positioning candles, flowers and carrying platters of condiments, veggies, dips, cheese and crackers from the kitchen.

Lastly, they place a narrow table next to the open doorway and set up an improvised bar, placing ice buckets and bottles of liquors, wines and mixers around them, As they work on this, Liz tells Mary about Kip's wounded foot, the new veterinarian, seeing Dan Parker, and finding the broken whiskey bottle. "Oh yes, we also got a couple of prank phone calls. What a jerk that guy must be to pull something so asinine."

Mary listens without comment until Liz tells about the phone calls and then she shouts, "Whoa, just a minute. Did you say you got prank calls that whistled into the phone? Hell, we got one just like that late last night. Then this morning, Larry went out to sweep the drive and found broken glass scattered over the driveway."

"What do you think is going on? Could this be more than just local kids?" Liz asks. "The half bottle I found had a horrible jagged edge and still reeked of whisky of some sort. So it has to have been put there recently. It's such a mean looking thing. I'm sure it was placed along the beach path on purpose. Kip says he recognized a scent like that of Dan Parker on it. However, it's hard for me to believe Dan would do something so mean spirited and stupid."

"I don't know what to think of that man. His actions last year shocked both Larry and me," Mary says. "Have you or Kip noticed anyone around your place? The way our houses are with your woods between us, we could miss seeing anyone coming and going down your road. Maybe we should set up security cameras on the fronts and backs of both houses. We'll have to ask if any of the others coming tonight have seen anything. Remind me to ask when I give the welcoming and toast. Maybe they've had things happen, too."

Before Liz can answer Mary, a deep voice calls out from the near end of the deck, "Hello there, Mary. Liz? I was hoping I'd find you here. I thought I'd come out to see how Kip's foot is doing. How are you, Mary? Hey, Larry? Good to see you're all here. It's been a long time since we've gotten together."

Both women turn to the voice expecting to see one of the invited neighbors and are stunned to silence when they see that the man walking towards them is non-other than Dr. Dan Parker. Without hesitating, Parker walks towards them as he continues talking to them, "Hey lucky me. It looks as if I'm in time for a drink and maybe an invite to dinner. Are you having a party? Would you mind if I stayed? What do you say, Liz? Would that be alright with you and Mary? Larry, it's good to see your still cooking. I just invited myself to your dinner party. How about giving me a drink?"

Having just come from the grill, Larry stands openmouthed in front of the three people holding a large stainless steel pan with the smoking roast on it. Both women can see the poor man is stunned to see the other man standing on his deck. Trying to cover up his surprise, Larry stutters his answer quickly, too quickly, "Aahh-mmm, sure, sure, old man, sure. Mix yourself a stiff drink. Make one for me. A G&T. Yeah, that'd be good. Sure, sure, stay for dinner. That is, if you can get past these two bulldogs named Mary and Liz. They're the ones you'll have to get the okay from. They make all the decisions. Now you'll have to excuse me, I've got to put this meat in kitchen."

Staring at the man who'd brushed them off so completely a year ago, the two women turn to watch Larry scurry into the house with his load of smoking meat. Even when they can no longer see him, the two women stare at where he disappeared into the house for several more seconds. Finally, it's Mary who turns to Dan Parker with a frown covering her face and says, "What the hell, Dan, why not stay for dinner. You'll make a good addition to the seating arrangements. We're giving this dinner to introduce three new year-round neighbors.

"There's a lovely gentleman named Rudy Sloan that bought the house next to Liz's. I've made her in charge of making sure he's comfortable and well fed. However, there are two single ladies, about your age, who bought the last two houses by the cliffs and plan to live full time at Redcliff's Beach. Your job will be to host those two ladies. As I said, I've appointed Liz to keep Rudy Sloan entertained. Yeah, I am Liz. Okay, Dan, stay for dinner and keep the new ladies happy. That'll be your payment for your chow. Just know that after seeing you at your office, Liz has decided she is definitely immune to whatever charms you used on her last year. In fact, if I were you, I'd stay clear of her."

When her friend says this, Liz erupts with joyous laughter and says, "Oh, thank you, thank you, Mary, my dear, dear friend. Yes, indeed, Danny-boy, you listen to dear Mary. Stay for dinner, if you must, but know you are the gigolo of the evening. Bless you, Mary, you're so on target about everything."

Seeing the man's unease, Liz knows she's hit on the reason he came and says, "I wonder, Danny-boy, was it you that made a phone to the

Jackson's last night and two to my home this afternoon? Were you trying then to catch us at home?"

As soon as she asks, Dan Parker's face flames bright red and Mary bursts out laughing, "That was you? I wondered if it were. Why would you pull that kind of stupid kid stuff prank? Lordy, Dan, I thought you were rude last year when you left us sitting at Liz's without a single word of goodbye or see you later. Now, if it was you who made those phone calls, I think you're plain crazy. Really, man, tell us, are you crazy or are you just a weirdo? Huh? Dan?"

Before Dan reacts or tries to answer, Larry comes back from the kitchen and says, "Mary, would you prop open the oven door? It won't stay open for me. I want to let the meat rest for an hour before I cut into it. Hey, Dan, didn't the girls make you a drink? What would you like? A gin and tonic? That's your drink, isn't it? Dan? In fact, I'll make two as I'm ready for a good one. Liz? What would you like?"

Neither women say a word as Larry goes to the makeshift bar and begins to pour liquids into glasses. When he turns back holding a drink in each hand, the three silently stare at him and he says, "Well? How about it? Let's get on with the party."

As if given his cue to leave, Dr. Dan Parker spins on one foot, charges down the steps and runs around the corner of the house. Unable to hold back one more second, Liz begins to giggle loudly and is immediately joined by Mary. Soon the two women are laughing so loud and so hard they have to sit down on one of the benches beside the first long table.

Watching them with a puzzled look, Larry finally shouts, "Hey you two, stop that. What's the matter with you? What happened to Dan? What happened? Did I say something to him? Hey, Mary? Liz? Stop and tell me what's going on."

Holding their sides, both women struggle to stop their laughter. Finally, they are able to slowly control their laughter by not looking at each other. Frowning at the women, Larry asks, "What the hell happened? What did you do to poor Dan?"

When Larry says this, the two women erupt into another fit of laughter. Screaming and screeching, they shake their heads and wave at Larry to go away. Instead, he stands glowering at the women now grasping their stomachs and taking deep breaths.

Finally it is Mary who manages to get control of herself and she turns to tell Larry what happened with Dan Parker. Then adds, "I know Dan didn't admit that he made those phone calls, Larry, but when Liz asked him directly if he did, he turned beet red. Then, I asked why he would ever do such a stupid childish prank and he never once denied making the calls. It was then that you came from the grill. I could have hugged you for interrupting us. However, you stood there with that hunk of smoldering meat, completely oblivious to what had gone down."

Larry shakes his head, "I sure understand now why Dan didn't seem to have made any friends before he met us. The man is weird."

Nodding, Liz adds, "His reaction shocked the hell out of me. I thought he'd make a joke out of it. When he blushed, he knew he'd given himself away. That's why I started to giggle and then you asked why we hadn't made him a drink."

"And told him to join your dinner party," Mary snaps at her husband.

"Hey, what else could I do? Suddenly there the man was, big and live and smiling. Damn the guy, he can be charming, to say the least. He looked so darned interested in what I was doing that I almost demonstrated my basting technique. All he had to do was ask. Hey, am I hearing you straight? Are you two saying Dan made those strange phone calls? Then why the hell would he show up here and ask to stay for dinner?"

Liz shrugs her shoulders and says, "Who knows, Larry. Maybe he needed to see how disturbed we were by them. His own reactions gave him away. I've never seen any adult turn so red with guilt before. What do you think, Mary?"

"I think we can kiss Dan Parker off our lists and I'll be very surprised if he ever comes back to this end of the beach again."

In unison, Larry and Liz say, "We can only hope."

# TWO

*June 1st—Beth*

BETH reaches the granite slab below the north cliffs just before sunrise and runs across the huge rock to stand before the glowing golden stone within the cliff face. Putting her right hand onto the large protruding stone, she thinks back over the times she come to this place and murmurs, "Every morning of my life here at Redcliff's Beach I've run up to you, ever since Dad built his cabin."

Standing very still, she waits for any messages that might come through the stone to her. When nothing comes to her, Beth pulls her hand back, slaps the surface of the golden stone and shouts, "I declare this run good and done."

Turning to face the beach, Beth fully expects to see that she is in Ann Anderson's dimension. Instead, the scene is one she has never seen before. Her Redcliff's Beach has a narrow strip of sand with low sculpted sand dunes. Now, the beach in front of her has high rolling sand dunes that stretch several hundred feet further before reaching the waves crashing against the point of the cliffs.

Shocked, Beth stares at the changes. Turning to face the high mountains to the east, she sees large, mansions, tucked within a densely forested hillside. Below these, she sees brick-walled road following the shoreline. "Of course, that would be the Shoreline Drive in this dimension. How else could each of these mansions to be reached."

Squinting against the rising sun, she sees each mansion is separated by acres of forest with wide winding driveways curving down the hillside to connect with this Shoreline Drive. As she stares at the beauty around her, it slowly occurs to Beth that she has seen nothing move. Not within the houses nor amongst the sand dunes nor flying through the air. There is only the soft wash of waves in the distance. No flicker of lights or scream of gulls, nothing. It's as if the homes, as well as the beach, have been abandoned.

Then Beth has a moment of panic and asks, "Am I deaf?"

Clapping her hands, she hears the sound of their impact and knows her hearing is the same as always. "Damn, I should have brought Dandy with me instead of letting her sleep on the golden stone under the table with Kip and Honey. Maybe I wouldn't have come through to this dimension if she'd been with me."

The thought of her large orange tabby cat brings a smile to Beth's face and she says, "Oh Dandy, when you hear where I've gone to today, you are going to be so jealous."

Slowly scanning the dunes to the south, she still sees no signs of life where hundreds of gulls and terns would have been on her own beach. "Why is there nothing? What caused this silence? There should be lights on in those houses. Instead, there is nothing alive on this beach... Nothing."

Shading her eyes with one hand, Beth squints at an oddly shaped house that slowly appears as the sun rises over the mountains tops. The oddity sits where her own cabin would be in her own dimension and she growls, "What the hell is that supposed to be? I see the cabin could be where that green roof shows on the lowest section. But what's that awful addition going up the hill? It goes almost to that road. Hey, wait a sec. isn't there something is moving down by that house? Yes, there is. I think it's a dog. Yes, a dog came from the cabin part. It seems to be coming this way. Hey, now a person running after it."

Watching what she assumes is a boy and his dog, she lets her eyes wander back to the long odd structure the two had come out from. The odd structure spreads up over the entire basalt flow where her own driveway is. Then she realizes something and exclaims, "That house is the only structure below the road for as far as I can see. All the other houses are tucked into the forested hillside as if by some mandate. I wonder why that is."

Staring down the beach, she realizes the boy and his dog are getting closer to her and seem to be running at a fast pace. Suddenly, the dog races ahead of the boy and she hears a distant whistle. At that, the dog turns back to wait for the boy and stays by his side.

"The child must have noticed me. I wonder if I should go meet him. No, of course not. The touchstone warned that we shouldn't wander into unknown dimensions. I've already been here longer than I should have. Guess I'd better go slap the touchstone again and get back home. If any Elizabeth Anns live in this dimension, they'll just have to come to the adjoined tables or the crystal room."

Standing next to the golden stone in the cliff face, Beth turns to look back at the person running to the cliffs. This time, she sees it is a teenage boy and that he is carrying what looks to be a stick and that he is running very fast, as if trying to reach her quickly. "Holy cow, at that speed he'll be here in minutes. Well, since he is not another Elizabeth Ann Anderson, it's time I slap the touchstone and get back home."

However, Even though she's told herself to do so, Beth watches the young man for a couple minutes more and says, "Is he running up to slap the touchstone? If that's so, maybe he knows another Elizabeth Ann."

No sooner than she says this aloud, then the boy stops, kneels on the sand and puts the long stick he carried up to his shoulder. In the next instant, Beth hears a zinging sound as something flashes past her left ear. Whatever it is smashes into the granite cliff with a sharp twang. A second later there is the loud cracking blast of a gunshot so loud it deafens her. Instantly, Beth whirls around to slap the touchstone, but before she can raise her hand to slap the glowing stone, the dog is standing next to her wagging its tail. Turning to see where the boy is, Beth sees he is again aiming his rifle at the cliffs.

Dropping flat onto the granite slab, Beth lands hard on the stone a split second before there is another twanging sound. Then, the dog yelps loudly and runs back to the boy. Without further hesitation, Beth jumps to her feet, slaps the touchstone hard and screams, "This run is good and done."

However, in the second it takes her to do this, before she enters her own dimension, something rips into the flesh of Beth's left arm. Clutching the wound, Beth feels a warm wetness and sees blood dripping onto the granite slab. Turning towards Lucy Wong's trailer parked on the roundabout at the end of Shoreline Drive and begins to scream for help. The lights and hum of a generator tells Beth that her friend is working under the green and white striped awning and she tries to scream louder, "Help me, Lucy, I've been shot. Help me."

Angered more than scared, Beth stumbles off the granite slab and stumbles across the narrow strip of sand before reaching the rip-rap boulders along the shoreline. It's this movement that catches Lucy's attention and, as Beth steps onto the tarred roundabout, Lucy see the blood dripping off Beth's left elbow and she demands, "Beth, what the hell happened to you?"

Wrapping her right arm around Lucy's shoulders, Beth lets Lucy half walk half carry her to the chairs under the trailer's green and white striped awning. Ignoring the sea life specimens spread across a long table, Lucy pushes Beth onto one of the chairs and demands, "Tell me what happened, Beth. It looks as if you've been shot. Who did this?"

Trying to focus on her friend, Beth says, "I went to an unknown dimension and some kid shot me. Lucky me, he was a lousy shot and missed twice. Third time he got me as I slapped the touchstone to come home."

As the words leave her mouth, Beth begins to shake uncontrollably. Holding her, Lucy lifts Beth off the chair and swings her around, then sets her down in one of the two chaise lounges a short ways from the work table. Then Lucy rushes into the trailer and returns with a first-aid kit and a wool blanket. Without a word, she rips the sleeve off Beth's shirt and begins to cleanse the hole in Beth's arm with hydrogen peroxide.

When the sting of the antiseptic over powers the pain of the wound, Beth begins to cry and says, "Damn it, Lucy, I couldn't tell if the person was a man or a woman until they got closer. Only then could I see it was a young man. He had a large red dog with him. It wagged its tail when it got to me. For some reason, I stood and watched that guy kneel and take aim at me. It all seemed so unreal that I couldn't believe what I was seeing. The damn guy shot three times. I was so lucky that he missed the first two times. I guess he was a lousy shot. That last one caught my arm at the moment I slapped the stone to return here.

"Oh crap. Lucy, I'm going to faint, no, I'm going to vomit "Aacckk…" As Beth vomits, Lucy thrusts a bowl holding cleaned uncooked clam specimens under her friend's chin. Grabbing it with her good hand, Beth vomits twice more than gasps, "Whew…ummm, uhh… Thanks, kiddo. Lordy, what did I eat that smells so fishy?"

Grinning, Lucy says, "That's not your vomit, that my morning's fresh dug specimens. The gulls will get it all after you're through vomiting into it. Are you done? Good. I'll go get you a clean bowl to keep on your lap in case you're not through upchucking. Then I'll finish with that wound. I need to see how bad it is. If it's clean, I can bandage it. If the bullet's still inside, I'm taking you into the ER and you get to explain how you got it."

"Thanks for the bowl and quick thinking. Though, I may never eat clams again though, whew… what a smell." Beth says, then falls silent as Lucy pours peroxide into the open hole wound in her arm. For the next several minutes, Beth silently watches Lucy poke at the wound and, when she begins to cover the opening with gauze, vomits one more time into the clean bowl on her lap. Finally, Lucy wraps the gauze with tape and gathers up the first aide items.

Seeing her do this, Beth tries to smile at Lucy as she says, "Thanks for your good work, my friend. Can I sit here for a while before I head home? I'm a still shaky."

"Yes, my friend, I insist that you do. Lay back and close your eyes. Take a nap. When you waken, I'll fix lunch and, only if I think you're up to being home alone, I'll drive you there. Okay?"

"Thank you so much, Lucy. Would you like to hear what I saw on that beach?"

"Yes, I would. However, if you feel like nodding off, let yourself go. I'll wake you up when lunch is ready."

"Alright… Let's begin at the beginning…that other Redcliff's Beach was absolutely beautiful. The sand dunes were ten to twelve feet high down past the granite slab and continued a good half mile out past the point before they touched the waves. There were no sounds. Nothing moved. Not a single shorebird flew past me or around the cliff tops. None anywhere. It was a terrible silence, so eerie…." With these last words, Beth slips into a deep sleep.

Lucy hears the thickness in Beth's speech and quickly goes over to lower the chaise lounge into a flatter position. Then she raises the other end by putting one of the folding chairs under it so Beth's feet are higher than her head. Then Lucy checks the bandaged arm for any excessive bleeding and whispers to Beth, "You're a damn lucky lady, Beth. That bullet went clear through and the bleeding cleaned out the wound. You rest now. I'll be working close if you need anything, just ask."

An hour later, Beth moans loudly and moves her legs as if running. Then she raises her arms to cover her face and screams, "No. Don't do that. Nooo..." and sits up yelling, "Why the hell did you do that?"

Reacting quickly, Lucy rushes to her and says, "You're safe, Beth, you're here with me. I'm Lucy Wong and you're safe here with me. You were shot by a boy in another dimension. But now you're home with me. Stop pulling at the bandage on your left arm or you'll open your wound again. Lie still. I'll get some meds. Close your eyes. I'll be right back."

Rushing into her trailer, Lucy returns in seconds with a glass of water in one hand and two pills in the other. Touching Beth's hand with the cool glass, Lucy waits until her friend opens her eyes, then says, "Here, dear, take a sip of this water. Now swallow these two painkillers.

I'll give you a couple more to take around nine tonight. Now sleep. I'll wake you for lunch. You can tell me what you saw and who shot you."

Beth gives a sleepy grin and says, "Okay, doc, I'll tell you later."

At that, Beth closes her eyes and doesn't open them again until nearly noon when Lucy touches her and says, "Wake up, sleepyhead. Lunch is ready."

Opening her eyes, Beth turns her head to see Lucy standing beside her with a bucket in one hand. The long table is now set with plates of food and glasses filled with water. Trying to speak, Beth can make only a low noise in her throat. That tickles her throat and causes her to cough loudly.

Looking down at her sleepy-eyed friend, Lucy hands her a glass of water and says, "Welcome back, kiddo. Drink this. Do you remember why you're there on the chaise under my awning? No? Well, I'm not going to tell you. Just lie still and let things come back to you. I'm going to go empty the scrap bucket at the edge of the waves. When, I get back I'll bet you'll be able to tell me what happened. If you haven't remembered by then, I'll tell you what you told me. Okay?"

Nodding, Beth closes her eyes and lets her mind go back to her morning run to the touchstone. She sees herself running across the granite slab, slapping the touchstone and yelling "I declare this run good and done." Suddenly all that happened after that comes rushing into her head and she sees it play out as if a film running under her eyelids, the new dimension's magnificent mansions, the odd building a mile down the beach and the dog and a person running up the beach. Again, she hears a shot and the second as each smashes into the cliff face. When she slaps the golden stone, she feels the bite of a third shot ripping through the flesh of her left arm.

Raising her arm, she looks at the bandage, pulls at it and gasps as pain shoots down to her fingers. That's when she realizes how gentle Lucy was when she cleaned and wrapped the wound with the gauze bandage. Forcing herself into a sitting position, Beth tosses the wool throw off her legs and shifts them off the side of the lounge.

Looking down at, she sees Lucy heave the contents from the

specimen bucket into the waves. Instantly, dozens of seagulls flap down and scream their delight at the easy meal. Running back to the roundabout, Lucy sees Beth sitting on the side of the chaise and says, "Those damn birds see me with this bucket and they know its meal time. Look at that mob go after it. Guess I'll have to take it down to the south cliffs and toss the goods out there."

Seeing Beth smile, Lucy nods and says, "Yes, yes, I remember you said I should do that when I came here last year." Holding out her hand to Beth she says, "Come on. Let's eat before those birds decide to take the food off our plates. Are you feeling better?"

Nodding, Beth answers, "I guess I do. Though I feel about half here. Would that be from the pills you gave me or from being shot?"

"Probably the pills. Their potency keeps normal people quiet for several hours and you only slept for three. However, I've never been shot, so it could be the trauma that has you reeling. While we eat, tell me what happened. Okay?"

"Will do. However, before I do, I need to pee. Will you help me inside?"

Lucy chuckles, "Come on. Tuck your right arm over my shoulder… that's it… good girl. One thing for sure, that function is a good sign your body's getting back to normal. Holler when you finish and I'll get you settled. Then I'll bring the food out, or would you rather eat inside?"

"Outside. Definitely."

After lunch is eaten and Beth has told Lucy all that happened in the other dimension, Lucy goes inside to wash dishes and finalize recording her morning's research. Beth lays back down on the chaise and is soon lulled to sleep by the waves slapping the north cliffs.

Suddenly the peace is shattered by shrill screams bringing both Lucy and Beth to their feet. Pointing down at the granite slab at the base of the north cliffs, Lucy shouts, "Isn't that Ann? Beth? Isn't that your friend, Ann, on the granite slab?"

"Yes. Yes, it is." Beth cries as Lucy races to and through the rip-rap and splashes through the waves of the incoming tide to get to the granite slab where Ann is slumped below the golden touchstone. Clutching at

Lucy with her left hand, Ann sobs, "Help me, Lucy. Help me. Help me. I've been shot. Help me."

"I'm here, Ann, I'm Lucy. Beth is up at my trailer. She was also shot."

"Let her help you, darling, let Lucy bring you through those waves." Beth yells as she moves towards the rip-rap boulders. Going too fast, she stumbles and falls onto her knees. The hard packed gravel of the roundabout buries into her skin and she hisses through clenched teeth, she says, "Yeow…Oooweew. Damn damn damn. Damn."

Ignoring, Beth's dramatics, Lucy wraps her arms around Ann and half carries half pulls the woman into and through the rush of incoming waves. When they get up to the rip-rap, she leads Ann between the huge boulders and of the rip-rap. As soon as she is through the roundabout, Lucy turns to Beth and scolds, "Damn it, Beth, you should have stayed on the chaise. You'll just have to wait for me to doctor those knees. Ann comes first. She got shot in some dimension as you did."

Looking at Lucy with a terrified expression, Ann exclaims, "Beth got shot in another dimension? Dear God, that's what happened to me. I went into an unknown dimension and some teenager and his dog were sitting on the granite slab. When he turned and saw me, he yelled, 'Momma, why don't you stay here with me? Why do you keep going away? Please, come back. Please, stay here with me. I'm so sorry that I shot at you a while ago. Please stay with me.' Then he started to climb onto the granite with a rifle and it fired a shot at me. I was close to the touchstone and slapped it. Oh, Lucy, I thought I was dead. I really thought I was dead."

As the two move slowly cross the turnaround, Beth shuffles closely behind them and Lucy snaps, "Beth, go get the first aid kit while I get Lucy settled on the chaise lounge. It's on the inside table. Hurry."

Ignoring the pain in her knees, Beth does as she is told and when she comes out with the kit, Lucy has Ann tucked into the chaise lounge where Beth had been sitting. Pulling a chair from the table over beside the lounge, Lucy sits next to Ann and asks, "Can you slip your shirt off? That's okay, I'll cut it off. Beth lost a sleeve from hers. Sorry, I have to do this, Ann. But the damage to you seems to be on your right shoulder.

Stop pulling away. I've got to cut the shirt off to see what the damage is. You're only making it hurt more."

When Beth lays the first aid kit on the lounge beside her, Ann sees the thick bandage on Beth's upper left arm and says, "Oh Beth, are you alright? Lucy told me you got shot too. I'm so sorry, darling. Are you alright now?"

Taking the pair of scissors from the kit, Lucy carefully snips off Ann's shirt on the right side. Seeing her flinch, Lucy says, "Ann, while I'm cleaning your wound, tell Beth what happened to you. Maybe you two can figure out if you were in the same dimension and got shot by the same boy. Okay, take a deep breath and brace yourself, Ann. I'm going to pour hydrogen peroxide over this wound to cleanse it. It's stopped bleeding and looks more like a deep scratch. Not too deep. I won't have to take you into the clinic. Beth was also lucky, her bullet went clear through so I was able to care for her wound here. But I'm not a medical doctor, so you both have to react to any changes in temps or colorations and get yourself to the ER. Do you both understand?'"

Helping Ann unbutton and strip off the rest of her shirt, Beth says, "Lucy is right. It looks more like a deep scratch across the top of your right shoulder. She is also right about our being two of the luckiest women that kid's a lousy shot."

After she says this, Beth kisses the top of Ann's head and holds her gently as Lucy finishes dressing the wound. Sighing, Lucy nods and says, "Yes, you're both right. That kid is a lousy shot or he didn't intend to kill either of you. I think it's more interesting that you both went into the same dimension on the same day."

Ann frowns at Lucy and says, "Yes. I was thinking that, Lucy. What's the reason that boy shot us? He kept calling me Mom. Could that Redcliff's Beach have another Elizabeth Ann Anderson living there?"

"You say the boy called you Mom before he dropped his rifle? I don't remember him saying anything to me. But why shoot you if he thought you were his mother?"

"Whatever the reason, I'm so glad that he didn't kill either of you. Okay, brace yourself, Ann, I'm pouring more peroxide on your wound then I'm going to wrap it. Then, I want you both to rest here for at least an hour. After that, if you feel up to it, I'll drive you down to Beth's. Okay?"

Wincing as the hydrogen peroxide is poured onto her wound, Ann grimaces until the stinging cleanse runs its course. When it does, she speaks softly as if thinking aloud, saying "That kid was sitting on the edge of a granite slab just like the one down here. His dog saw me first and wagged its tail as if it knew me. When it came over to me, the boy turned and called me Mom. I must look a lot like his mother and he thought I had come back to him."

As Lucy gently lays a thick gauze pad over the four inch path caused by the bullet, Ann groans loudly. Taking her good hand in hers, Beth says, "Hang on, sweetheart, it only hurts for a little while. Lucy has a pain pill that'll make you feel much better. In fact, it'll make you very sleepy. We both have to thank Lucy for being here and for that boy for being such a lousy shot."

"Yes, we do." Ann nods. "He said, 'Mom, why do you keep coming back? Don't you realize you're dead? Why do you keep coming back?' That's when I hit the touchstone and shouted our mantra at the same moment and he dropped the rifle. I guess when I think about that, he didn't mean to shoot at me, the rifle shot me. Thank God, Honey stayed in my cabin with Kip and Dandy on the golden agate, so she wasn't with me."

"Yes, I saw the three of them there when I left for my run. They often come together even when you and Liz aren't there. It seems our animals have strong connections to each other that don't include us. Lucy, dear? Would you drive Ann and me down to my place right now? I want to make certain Dandy is there. If so, can you give Ann a couple of your magic pills? They'll make her sleep and I could use another long nap. I'm completely washed out."

"Of course, I'll get my purse and keys. You two go climb into the truck. Be sure to take the other pills later tonight. That way you'll have a good night's sleep."

# THREE

## *June 1ˢᵗ—Ann*

**ANN** reaches over to the right side of the bed to touch Beth and pain shoots through that side of her body and she shouts, "Beth? My shoulder is killing me. What the hell did you do to me last night?"

In that instant, she realizes she is no longer in Beth's bedroom but back in her own dimension and in the bed within her small cabin on the basalt point. Slowly turning over to her left side, Ann manages to sit up and swing her legs off that side of the bed. Looking around, she sees the wonderful small cabin she built over the section of the polished cement floor left from her Dad's cabin last year.

When she sees the golden stone under the adjoined table, her Golden Retriever, Honey, is watching her. The big dog's tail wags so hard it thuds against one of the table legs and Ann says, "Well, howdy girl. You've been here all the while I slept? Good girl."

In the next moment, the large dog bounds onto the bed and covers Ann's face with wet licks. "Gently, girl, gently... I got shot yesterday... or is it still today? Anyway, I have a wound on my right shoulder. I'm so glad you stayed here with Kip and Dandy. Beth got shot by the same boy. We both are lucky to be alive."

As if an answer, the large dog gives Ann's cheek another quick lick and she says, "Was it you that called me home? Or did I need to rest at home. Either way, I'm glad to be here with you. Going into that unknown dimension and getting shot was not something I ever want to do again. I hope that poor boy finds whoever he's looking for."

Its then that Ann hears these words in her head,

*He will know the truth soon. You must listen to his mother's essence when she comes to talk to you. Her words are what the boy needs to hear.*

Staring at the large Golden Retriever, Ann frowns, "Did you just tell me something, Honey? Were those words from you that I heard in my head?"

*Yes, dear. As Kip is to Liz, I am your animal familiar. I decided it was time for you to know who and what I am. I am here to be with you during the Summer Solstice you are going to experience. The Universe has plans for each of you and your others.*

For several seconds, Ann looks at the animal in disbelief. Finally, she says, "All right, smarty, if you know so much, tell me what happened to my shoulder. Why did that boy shoot at me?"

*He didn't mean to do so. He leaned the rifle against the edge of the granite slab and it fell over, then trigger got caught by a jagged piece on the stone. He did not aim the gun at you.*

As the animal's words fill her mind, Ann scrambles out from under the bedding and shouts, "What the hell are you? Am I really hearing words that come from your head to mine? Honey? Are you really telling me these things?"

*Yes, Ann, I am telling you these things, now hush. Enough with the hysterics. Calm yourself and listen to me. I have something important to tell you. In a few minutes, the essence of that boy's mother will be with you soon. She has tried several times to reach her son. However, she frightens him and he flees from her. Both you and Beth got shot because of that fear. Her human name was Elizabeth Ann Gardner and her son is named Neil. She is called Bette. Listen to her plea, then retell it to both Liz and Beth.*

*You each must know Bette is one of your Parallel Lives, so listen closely to what she says. One of you three must go into that dimension and tell Neil that his mother wants him to listen to her. She is going to tell you to say. Do you understand what I am telling you? Ann? Please, nod or say yes right now, as Bette is here by the adjoined table. See how bright the golden stone is glowing? That is its way of greeting known Universal entities.*

"I'm sorry, Honey. I find it so hard to believe you are really telling me these things. I do know what was said. I just can't believe that it is your words in my head. Is this how Kip talks to Liz?"

*Of course, it is, you ninny. Dandy talks to Beth the same way. Now, shut up and listen to Bette Ann Gardner, Neil's mother, her essence is here.*

Suddenly the small cabin is filled with brilliant light and moves towards Ann. Trying to sees the shape within the light, Ann says, "Honey, tell that thing her light is too bright. It's hurting my eyes. I can't look at her."

Immediately, the light dims and Ann sees a woman standing within a soft glow. Pulling Honey close to her side, Ann whispers, "Honey? Is that who wants to talk to me? Honey?"

*Yes. Be silent and listen.*

Then the dog lays down on the bed and Ann whispers, "Damnit, Honey, this is scarier than hell. Sit next to me and don't abandon me to whatever this is. Get up. Sit next to me. If that's what the mother shows to boy, I can see why he was so frightened when he saw her. She looks exactly like me. In fact she could be Beth or Liz, too. That's why Beth and I went in that dimension, she's another Parallel Life of Elizabeth Ann Anderson."

Saying that, Ann walks toward the image and says, "If you're Neil Gardner's mother, tell me what you want me to tell him. What are you saying? I'm sorry, I can't hear you. I see your mouth moving, but I can't hear a word you say. Are you Elizabeth Ann Anderson? Are you a Parallel Life from the original child having that name, Beth Anderson?"

Taking another step towards the image, Ann shouts, "I asked is your name Elizabeth Ann Anderson? What do you want to tell me?"

In response to her shout, a loud booming voice fills Ann's head making her shout, "Not so loud. Softer. Please. There, that's good. Yes. Now I hear what you're saying."

As Ann speaks to it, the image slowly comes into focus. Ann says, "I've been told you were Bette Gardner, Neil's mother. I can see you are another Elizabeth Ann Anderson, a Parallel Life of myself and the other Parallel Lives known as Beth Anderson and Liz Day. You're the reason why Beth and I went into Neil's dimension this morning. Do you understand what I mean?"

Immediately, Bette's image tells her,

*Yes, I understand. You and I were born as one with the original Elizabeth Ann Anderson. Our parents were the same people, James and Jill Anderson. Both of us came to Redcliff's Beach every year of our childhood. Our father, James Anderson, built his cabin on this same basalt flow where our cabins both stand. Both my parents died several years after yours did. Now I want to tell you about myself before I tell you what to say to Neil. Would you like to know about me?*

"Yes, of course, I would like to know about you, Bette and I'll tell the others when they come to the adjoined tables."

*My husband was Lewis Gardner. He and I expanded the cabin's footprint up the basalt flow. It is now a large expansive house where we entertained our large extended family and friends. Our home nearly reaches the road known as Shoreline Drive.*

*I worked as an actress and called myself Bette Anderson. After I married my husband, Lewis Gardner, I changed my last name to his as he was a very famous film director and doing so gave me much status. We had one boy child which we named Neil Allan. He is the boy whose rifle shot you and the other one called Beth, early this morning. I apologize for his doing that. Neil should have been more careful. However, he was very frightened by the events which took my husband's and my lives two years ago on the first of June.*

*I am sure Neil thought you were me and that he is sorry he shot either of you. I'm sure that he will never do it again. I tried to talk to Neil, but whenever I appear to him, my essence frightens him. Could you, or one of the other Parallel Lives, go into his dimension and demand that he go sit at the table over the golden stone? If he does go there, I will come to him. Tell him that he should not be frightened of me. He is my son and I love him.*

*Neil should be told that Lewis and I did not suffer when we were killed. I must tell him what happened and how to stay safe so that his life will continue.*

*He is destined to do great things for his country. Would one of your Parallel Lives go back to my dimension and tell him this for me?*

"It's too soon, Bette, I don't' think I can get back to your dimension so soon. Maybe Liz would be able to go through to talk to him. Liz is the one who brought us together two years ago. Her husband, Peter, came back and told her that her Parallel Lives were near her. At least she will know to be very cautious of Neil. What is he doing alone on that beach? Why carry the rifle?"

*The country was attacked while Neil was still in school taking his final exams for the year. It was the week before his summer vacation. Lewis and I were at the beach getting the house ready. On June first, we were one the deck watching a wonderful sunset. Suddenly dozens of planes came out from those brilliant colors and we stood waving at the formations as they flew over. Lewis and I were killed instantly.*

*We didn't know it was the Chinese Air Force. Did I say it was June first? Yes? It was, two summers ago. Many who lived along the West Coast were killed or badly wounded that day. Neil lives because he was still at his boarding school in Bozeman, Montana. Lewis and I work most of the year, but we keep our summers open to spend with Neil at Redcliff's Beach. He loves the beach and he loves the boarding school he chose in Montana as it encourages students to bring their pets with them. Reilly is Neil's Irish setter and the two of them are amazing together. Neil claims that Reilly talks to him. Now, I know that he does and is Neil's animal familiar.*

Ann smiles for the first time since Bette's essence had appeared and she says, "Now I understand. Poor Neil, he must be feel so alone and angry. Do you know why the Chinese invaded your country? We are close allies in my dimension. Why didn't your government know what was happening? How could all those planes make it to Redcliff's Beach without being caught on radar and intercepted? Don't you have radar?"

*They came from their planned and announced month long show of power. On the second month of May, the Chinese had their full navy out in the middle of the Pacific doing their maneuvers. At first everyone thought they were flaunting their military might and we watched it on the news each evening. However, when it went on so long, it got too normal and boring. People stopped watching* as did those who should have known better. After another two weeks, their wargames became a joke around the dinner tables and that's when Chinese came at us. It was a sneak attack right at sunset.

Lewis and I thought the planes were ours showing off our own military power. When we were in front of the Universal Counsel, we were told the Chinese wanted our flat farm land. They even told us that years before when President Chow visited our country and told the officials touring him how lucky we were to have such abundant farmlands. Everyone was pleased and no one heard the threat of his words. Besides, China was too far away to ever be a threat to our country.

After Chow's visit, the Chinese government quietly took control of several coral atolls in the South Pacific. Within a few years, they had formed a large chain of islands along the edge of the Pacific Rim. These new islands held communities for their people who built airports, shipping ports, huge warehouses and apartment houses. Soon, there was everything they needed for an invasion. Only the small nations around the area protested to the United Nations. Nobody with any power demanded the work be stopped.

The Chinese had narrowed the vast distance to the United States, Canada and Mexico. That first evening those planes killed with bullets and rockets. The several hundred were bombers which dropped bombs filled with poisonous gas that killed everything living within hundreds of miles. The third round of planes came immediately after that and flew inland. These were troop carriers which dropped thousands of paratroopers who were killed by the poisonous gas dropped earlier and still lay within the mountainous terrain.

"Did any gas reach other parts of the country? Is that why Neil and his dog are the only living thing on your beach?"

The initial attacks only reached the coastal states. When it was reported on the news, everyone across the country reacted. Neil's school was locked down immediately and, though it was dangerous, he took Reilly and left in his Jeep to come to us at the beach. Sadly, when he got here, he found Lewis's and my bodies on the front deck of our cabin and buried us under the water tower Dad built near Shoreline Drive.

President Ellen Boneau immediately declared war on Chine, called for all able bodied people to ready for an attack. Soon there were huge local militias all across the country, each person armed with their own guns. The local groups prepared to defend themselves from invader and criminal opportunists. It was this response by the citizens which stopped the advance of the Chinese invaders. Scattered through the Western states, they weren't prepared to face such quickly organized and armed forces. Since then, most have surrendered, though some are still hiding in the mountains. Those are what threaten Neil and must prepare himself to hide or fight.

The rifle Neil has was his Dad's gun. Last week, several Chinese came down from the mountains and stormed into the homes on Redcliff's Beach. Luckily, Reilly warned Neil and they hid under the deck around Dad's cabin. It was always a favorite place for the two of them. It was many years before he knew his Dad and I would go under there when he went back to school. Because of this space, he and the dog slip out at night and pick off stray enemy soldiers.

The week after the attack, President Boneau sent ships and planes to drop bombs on each of the seven islands. Three of the bombs were atomic bombs and those islands are no more.

"My God, Bette, how did the rest of the world react to that? Did the people demand that she be recalled?

No, she was hailed as a heroine by the world as all knew she made the necessary decision in response to that horrendous attack. China is now isolated from the rest of the world. The terrible war is over and our soldiers are searching everywhere for the last of the enemy. There are several in the Coastal mountain range. That's why Neil was so frightened the day he saw you. He didn't know if you were friend or foe until he got close enough. Then he saw you looked like me and it scared him.

Neil has buried the dead by himself. The animals and birds he take out on the sands at low tide and let the ocean carry them away. The poor boy has been so traumatized, that I fear for his mental health. That's why I must speak to him. Would you or one of the others go tell him to sit at the table over the golden stone and wait for me to come to him there? I must talk to him.

He replenishes his food supply from the other homes on Redcliff's Beach and that puts him in great danger from both from the enemy and our own armed services who might see his taking things from another house as being a criminal. His terrified reaction to the appearance of you and Beth shows how much he *needs my help. Please, tell him to sit at the table over the golden stone in and I'll come to him there. I must talk to him.*

"I'll tell Liz and Beth what you told me as soon as you leave. I promise. One of us will get through to Neil."

As Ann says these last words, the vision of Bette Gardner fades until it vanishes from the room. Shaken by what Bette told her, Ann goes directly to the adjoined table and sits on her chair and says, "Honey, come lay on the golden stone and call Kip and Dandy to come through to us and bring Liz and Beth with them. They must hear what Bette told me, right now."

While Honey settles onto the golden stone under the table, Ann silently meditates on bringing her Parallel Lives to the adjoined tables. A few minutes later, Honey's tail begins to wag and Ann can see both Kip and Dandy beside the golden stone. Within minutes, both Beth and Liz appear on their chairs at the adjoined tables and tears fill Ann's eyes as she exclaims, "Thank you both for coming through to me so quickly. I have so much to tell you. I met a new Elizabeth Ann Anderson. Her name is Bette Ann Gardner and she was the mother of Neil Gardner, the young man who shot at us, Beth. She told me a shocking story about what happened to her and her husband Lewis. Please sit here with me and listen closely. Here's what she told me…"

Ann repeats Bette's story to Beth and Liz and the two women are silent until she finishes. Then, Beth says, "I was so worried when you vanished from my bed this morning. Now I understand why you were brought back here. Someone needed to hear Bette's story. Thank you for telling us so quickly. We now know that poor boy has gone through hell and I agree with Bette, one of us must get back to that young man and tell him what she said. He must hear what she told Ann."

As Beth finishes her statement, both Liz and Kip vanish from inside Ann's cabin. Surprised by the sudden disappearance of the other two, Beth says, "Well, I guess that's all Liz needed to hear. I wonder if it means she'll be the one to go into Neil's dimension. Our own injuries may keep us away from that dimension until they heal. How are you feeling? Would you like me to make us some dinner? I'd like to hear more about the vision you saw and what else she said about the boy?"

"Yes, please stay. I'm sorry I vanished from your bed without a word. I'm not even sure when it happened. In fact, I'm not sure what day this is. Is it the same day we got shot?"

"Yes, it is, my darling. Why don't I take out that meatloaf and make us a couple of hot sandwiches. Then let's walk down to the top of your cliff tops and watch the sunset."

# FOUR

*June 5<sup>th</sup>—Liz*

**LIZ** and Kip reach the huge granite slab at the base of the north cliffs and Liz helps Kip onto its flat surface. "Does your paw hurt at all?"

*No, dear one, it feels good. I'm so glad to be at the touchstone again. Where are we going today?*

"I thought we should try again for Neil's dimension. It's been almost a week since his mother's essence asked Ann to help her. Are you sure you up to that kind of adventure?"

*Yes. Let's try for it again. That boy needs to hear what his mother wants him to know. What else would be so good?*

Liz asks, "We could go to the crystal room. It's been a couple weeks since we were last there."

*Yes, that would be good, too. Maybe Honey and Ann will be there.*

Just as Liz raises her hand to slap the touchstone, a volleyball bounces against the cliff face and Kip jumps to bounce his nose against it. As it rebounds off the cliff face, the youth running after the ball catches it and yells, "Hey guy you're good. We could use you on our team." Laughing at his joke, the youth tosses the ball back to another player on the court being setup on a section of sand several yards from the base of the cliffs.

Chuckling, Liz tells Kip, "I'll bet that kid would drop dead if he knew exactly how good you are at nearly everything." Then she slaps the touchstone and shouts, "I declare this run good and done."

Instantly, Liz and Kip are transported to another dimension where there are high deep sand dunes that stretch far to the south. When she turns to the west, she sees the dunes stretch hundreds of feet past the granite slab before touching the waves of the incoming tide. When she starts to tell Kip something, she hears,

*Quiet. Don't say a word. Stay silent and don't move. This is the beach Beth and Ann told about. This is the dimension where they were both shot at by some kid. Look to your right, where the slab meets the cliff face. Do you see the boy?*

Liz looks where Kip said and sees the top of a blond head as a large red dog stands up and points at them. Frowning at Kip, Liz waits for him to tell her what to do next.

*That's only Reilly. He's my old friend. Do you see the boy's head and that gun beside him? Can you get it from him?*

Liz doesn't answer, but moves silently to the right side of the granite and stares down at a sleeping youth. Only the top of his blond hair shows above the edge of the slab. Leaning against the granite slab, poking just above the rock's edge is the shaft of a slim rifle. When she sees this, Liz realizes that if Kip hadn't been with her, she would never have noticed the boy. As she starts to bend over the youth, Kip says,

*Liz, this is my old friend Reilly.*

Without a sound, Kip trots over to the dog and touches noses with it. Each dog wags its tails and sniffs the other from head to tail, then standing in front of the other they seem to communicate without a sound for several seconds.

Waiting for Kip to tell her what to do next, Liz watches the dogs enjoy their renewed friendship. Finally, Kip says,

*Liz pick up the rifle by the shaft and lift it away from him. Reilly says the boys needs all the sleep he can get.*

Moving cautiously, Liz grabs hold of the rifle shaft, lifts it with both her hands and carries it back to stand in front of the touchstone. As she leans against the cliff face, she hears Kip say,

*Good girl. Now stay next to the golden stone. Now say Hi to my old friend, Reilly. He's going to wake his master. We'll stay here by the touchstone and the rifle and watch. When he's fully awake, you can talk to him.*

When she hears this, Liz makes certain the safety on the rifle is on, then she removes the clip full of bullets from the handle and the lone bullet in the chamber. When that is done, she stuffs the clip and bullet into her jacket pockets and carefully lays the rifle under the touchstone. Then she slips down to sit beside Kip and leans against the cliff face. Then she says loudly to the two dogs, "Okay, boys, wake the kid and tell him what he is to know."

*Consider it done.*

At that time, the red dog goes across the granite slab and licks at the young man's face until the boy's eyes flash open. Seeing Reilly above him, he groans, "Stop that Reilly. Why are you waking me? I haven't slept so well in days."

When the dog woofs and walks over to stand beside Liz and Kip, the boy immediately throws himself onto the sand and scrambles onto his knees behind a group of boulders next to the cliff face. After several seconds of silently scanning the sand for the rifle, he looks up to see Liz standing over him, holding the rifle over her head. Smiling at the youth, she says, "Looking for this?"

At that time, Kip barks three times and the youth falls flat to the sand. After a minute or so, Liz says, "For heaven's sake, Neil, stand up and come sit on the edge of the granite by Reilly. Good. Now, turn and face me. We need to talk. Kip, you and Reilly watch him. Take him down and pin him if he starts to run again."

Even as the young man sits beside his dog, he holds his hands high over his head. When he finally looks over at Liz, she sees his eyes are filled with fear and never leave the rifle laid across her lap. "Don't even think about making a move for your gun," she tells him.

"W-what are you going to do with me? You aren't my mom are you? I didn't mean to shoot at you. Not the second time, at least. Not really the first time, either. I didn't. It just happened. All I wanted was for you to stay where you were and talk to me. The first time, I thought you might be a Chinese soldier and I was scared. The second time I knew you weren't but you looked so much like my mother and I wanted to hold her to me. I didn't mean to shoot at you that time. My rifle slipped against this edge here on the granite. I just wanted so much to talk to you. You're my Mom, aren't you?"

Determined not to frighten the boy any more than he already was, Liz says, "No, Neil, I'm not your mother. My name is Liz Day. I'm from a totally different dimension. I have come from there to your dimension to give you a message from your mother, Bette Ann Gardner. I am not one of the two women you shot. I am a good friend of theirs. We are Parallel Lives of one child named Elizabeth Ann Anderson. The two women you shot were Beth Anderson and Ann Anderson. They wonder why you would shoot at a person who looks like your mother."

Frowning at Liz, the boy sputters, "How do you know about my mother? Who are you anyway? Why doesn't my mother come to me if all of you can do it?"

"Your mother has come to you Neil, but each time she does, you run away from her. That's why I'm here today. I was asked by your mother to tell you about what happened to her and your father, Lewis Gardner. They were killed by bullets from airplanes flown by the Chinese Air Force, two years ago. It was her essence which appears to you here in your dimension and it was her essence which appeared to Ann in her home, the same day you wounded her. That was nearly one week ago. Your mother's essence asked Ann to come to you and tell you to meet her at the table over the golden stone in the floor of your Grandfather's original cabin.

Bette Ann also wants you to apologize for shooting Ann and Beth. You were very lucky that your shots only wounded them. Bette told Ann about how the Chinese invaded your country and killed both her and your father when they flew over the beach. She wants you to know that both of your parents died quickly and never felt pain or knew what happened.

"Bette said she has tried to talk to you but you run away from her. You are to go to the adjoined table in the cabin where the golden stone in in the floor and wait there for her to come to you. Bette said she must tell you things that you need to know. Be there at sunrise and wait for her there. She will come to you. Do you understand, Neil?"

"My mother talked about me? How can that be? She's dead. So is my Dad. I buried them both under the water tower. How do you know about them? Where do you come from? How did you know my name is Neil? Maybe I'm called Earl.

Smiling at the youth, Liz says, "No, Neil. Your name is Neil Gardner and I already told you that I'm called Liz Day. I was born Elizabeth Ann Anderson, just as your mother was. I'm one of several Parallel Lives which split off the original child named Elizabeth Ann Anderson. The others I told you about are the women you shot at a week ago. They are also Parallel Lives of Elizabeth Ann Anderson, just as your mother was. This is my dog named Kip. He is my friend and my animal familiar just as your dog Reilly is your friend and your animal familiar. I learned all of these things from what your mother's essence told Ann. That's why I know your name is Neil."

Tears spring from the youth's eyes and rolled down his cheeks as he answers, "Yesss... that is my name. My mother looked exactly as you do, Liz. My folks worked hard most of the year, all over the world. Every summer we'd come here to the beach to be together. My mother's father, James Anderson built his cabin down where you see that long house, on the beach. He built the cabin for his family. The cabin part is still there where that greenish colored roof shows. If you squint, you can see it at the bottom of that long house about a mile south of here. The cabin is the part at the bottom and the part that goes up to Shoreline Drive was added on by my folks. My folks are... were... in the movie business and traveled a lot.

"When I was little I had a nannies and lived in a large house in Portland, Oregon. When I got into school, I got to choose the one I wanted to go to. I chose a super neat prep-school in Montana. They let us kids bring our pets with us. I brought Reilly with me when he was only a pup. Now look at him. He's a beauty, isn't he? Yeah you are, Reilly and you take good care of me."

Then the youth stops and looks at Liz for a long while before he continues, "You haven't told me where you came from."

"Actually I have, Neil, you just haven't listened to what I said. Let me try to explain it better. There are three of us who are Parallel Lives of the same child. Your mother makes it four. We each look exactly like the others. We each live in separate dimensions. There was a fifth one named Eliza Staples but she was killed. We three who are alive have known of each other for two years. We each accept the fact that each of us came from one child named Elizabeth Ann Anderson, the youngest child of Jim and Jill Anderson and accept that Beth Anderson was that child.

"When she was very young, Elizabeth Ann and her family were in a terrible accident. It was at that time each of our child essences split from the original Elizabeth Ann and fled through the Universe to separate dimensions. Each of us, our new Elizabeth Ann's, brought the entire world they loved with them. Everything, all the things they knew and loved, came with them.

"None of us felt this drastic change of dimensions. None of us were aware of the others. We three only met two years ago when each of us experienced a terrible trauma of losing our dearest loved one. That was on June first, the same day your parents were killed. That was the same June first. After we saw each other, it was impossible to deny we weren't of the same child. We could see that we each looked exactly like the others. Also each of our homes was the cabin James Anderson built for our family.

"Soon we realized that our dimensions were connected to each other at the exact point of the golden stone in the cement floor of our father's cabin. Each of us claimed the space as our own and it took several meetings at the adjoined tables over the golden stone before we finally accepted each other for who we are, the Parallel Lives of Elizabeth Ann.

"The adjoined table is the place your mother demands that you meet her. You are to sit there at sunrise and wait for her to come to you. Do you understand that, Neil? Wait for her to come to you at the dining table and stay to talk with her. You must never run away from her again. Do you understand what I'm telling you? When I leave, you are too there and wait for her. Your mother wants to be with you very much. She said she will come to you very soon.

Frowning, the youth shouts, "How do you know about that?"

"I just told you, you stupid boy. Were you listening to what I was telling you? Understand these fact, my father was James Anderson. He was the same James Anderson who was your mother's father. My mother was the same Jill Anderson that was your mother's mother. Both are the same parents your mother had and who you knew as your Grandparents. I had a sister named Dana Marie Anderson. All my family died in the terrible car crash when I was fourteen. A drunk driver smashed into Dad's car and killed all of them. All except me."

"No way… that's my Mom's story. Did you know my Mom? Do you know where Aunt Dede is?"

"No, I didn't know either of them, Neil. Stop questioning everything I say. Just accept that I live within an entirely separate dimension than you do. However, I still live in the original cabin built by James Anderson for his family. I have run up to these cliffs every morning that I'm able to, just as your mother, Bette Ann, ran to these cliffs each morning she was here. Did she slap the golden stone in the cliff face and shout 'I declare this run good and done' every morning she's at the beach? Did you run to slap the touchstone with her? Do you still run up here?"

"Yes, I did. I do. So did my Dad. Even Reilly ran with me."

"I was sure about that, but I had to ask. That's all I'm going to say for now. Just know that the essence of your mother, Bette Ann, appeared to Ann Anderson and told Ann to tell Beth and me so that if one of us came through to you, we would give you her message. I have done this for her. Remember, Neil, meet her at the table over the golden stone in your grandfather's cabin. Be there early in the morning. Now do you understand?"

For several seconds only the silence of the empty sky and beach holds the boy's attention. Finally he says, "Yes. I will go and wait for her.

Tell those other ladies that I'm sorry I shot them and, if they come back, I'll tell them myself. Tell them I'm not really crazy."

"We don't think you are, Neil. You're just a scared boy. Here is the clip from your rifle. The rifle will stay with you. You may need it to defend yourself from any stray enemy soldiers. Take care of yourself, Neil. Tell your mother, I believe she is right about your doing great things for your country in the future. Kip and I must go for now. Stay safe."

After she says this, the young man begins to sob and Liz moves to put an arm around his shoulders. However, when her hand touches his shoulder, both she and Kip are back in their own dimension, standing on the red granite slab at the base of the north cliffs on their own Redcliff's Beach and sees a group of young people batting a volleyball over a net.

Looking south, she says to Kip, "Isn't it wonderful to be back on our own beach, Kip? Just listen to the screams of those kids and those silly gulls fighting over that dead fish. I'll never curse loud happy sounds again. Let's go home, Kip. Want to race me?"

As they trot next to each other, they turn up the trail through the dunes to the house and reach the top step together. Laughing, Liz hugs the dog and says, "Gosh it's so good to have you back to normal. I hated that you were so badly injured by that broken glass."

*I'll second that, darling Liz. It's good to feel normal again.*

Bending, Liz kisses the top of Kip's head and says, "You were the best patient ever, dear one. The very best."

Suddenly, a voice shouts from the dunes nearest the house, "Who goes there?"

Laughing, Liz shouts back, "Only the two of us. What're you up to?"

At that moment, Mary Jackson comes around the highest dune between their two homes and waves both her hands high over her head, shouting, "Wait for me, Liz, I've got something to tell you."

Waving her hands over her own head, Liz yells back at her, "So come on and I'll make us some tea."

Waiting in the open slider door, Liz watches Mary hurry to the steps up to the cabin's deck and thinks,

*We're so lucky to have Mary and Larry next to us. I wish you'd been here before Peter died, then you'd have known the woman who lived in their house before they did."*

*That person was evil.*

Liz looks at Kip and thinks,

*Okay, smarty, what is Mary going to tell us?*

*Dan Parker plans trouble.*

Liz opens her mouth to speak, but only has time to sputter "What?" before Mary wraps her in a warm hug then bends down to give Kip a quick hug and rub between his ears. "How lovely that my two most favorite beings in the whole world would stop at my beck and call."

"It's because we love you so much, kiddo. Now, tell us, what's up?"

"The infamous Dr. Dan Parker called a bit ago and asked Larry and me to meet him for dinner with tonight at The Shores on Discovery Bay. I accepted as I thought his next sentence would be 'and would you bring Liz.' But he didn't, so am I to assume you're not going to be there or are you?"

"Not even if he'd sent a dozen orchids and crawled here on his knees to ask me personally. That I can assure you." Looking down at Kip, she asks, "Am I wrong?"

*Nope. You are too wise.*

Surprised again by Kip's return, Liz laughs and repeats, "Kip says, 'Nope. You are too wise.'"

"Damn, I wonder what that snake in the grass has planned for us. He really gives me the creeps. I was so taken aback that all I said was that we would. However, I did decline when he offered to pick us up. I told him we'd drive ourselves. I was at least wise enough to do that?"

"Don't worry, Mary. Take it as it comes. Just don't accept any wooden nickels from the guy and tell Larry to keep his mouth zipped tight. Are those enough clichés to stop your worrying about it?"

"Yes, thanks, kiddo. You're a hell of a lot of help. But, I have an idea. Why don't you call up that handsome widower neighbor of yours to the south? Rudy Sloan? That charmer who hung on your elbow at our neighborhood gathering last week. He's such a nice guy and he's right next door to you. Go ask him out for dinner as a friendly gesture. Then the two of you come with Larry and me tonight. I'll bet Sloan would jump at the chance."

"Do what?" Liz shrieks with laughter. "Oh no, not on this short notice and not to anything Dan is involved with. But it's a good idea for a later date. Yeah, I'll do it some other time. Right now, I'm making us tea and cutting that coffee cake I pulled from the freezer this morning. Then I'll catch you up on the saga of the Elizabeth Anns. Interested?"

"Always." Mary answers as she follow Liz and Kip through the slider door and sits at the dining table as Liz puts the teakettle on the stove and Kip laps from his water bowl. Both stop what they're doing when the phone on the kitchen counter rings and Liz answers, "Hello? This is Liz."

The voice on the other end is deep and a bit too familiar and Liz frowns as her stomach muscles tighten, "Hello Liz. This is Dan Parker. I wondered if you'll be home tonight. I'd like to come over around seven to see you and Kip. We need to talk."

"No, Dan. I don't want you to come over here tonight at seven or any other time. I told you that at your office last week. There is nothing I have to say to you and there is nothing I want to hear from you. Whatever might have been between us is long gone. You killed whatever it was over a year ago. If you come here, tonight or any other time, Kip and I will greet you with great hostility. Stay away from us. Don't step onto my property or I will take out an injunction out on you. Do you understand? I have nothing to say to you and you have nothing I want to hear from you. Good bye."

That said, Liz hangs up the phone and Mary says, "What the hell is he trying to do? That's the same time he's supposed to meet Larry and me at the restaurant on the other side of Discovery Bay. Wait until Larry hears about this."

Liz nods, "That man is one strange bugger, that's for sure. Do you know what he's doing, Kip?"

*He's up to no good. Your response was right. Lock the house tight. We'll wait for him with your pistol. Okay?*

"Thanks, dear one. Kip says to lock up the house and we'll wait for him with my pistol. Tell you what, Mary, why don't you and Larry come for dinner tonight? Say around five? We'll have a lovely evening and all be here to greet Dan when he shows up. That way, he'll know we're on to him. He certainly can't be in two places at one time."

The Jackson's arrive at Liz's home around five and the three friends plus Kip go out on the deck for chat and drinks while Liz grills T-bone steaks. By six-thirty, the three have finished their meals, fed Kip sizable hunks from each steak and the two women clear the dishes as Larry slices the gorgonzola cheese and sets some crackers around the plate.

Its then that Larry says, "I think we should be inside when Dan comes. I don't want to be out where he could pick each of us off without us ever seeing him. I'm sure Kip wouldn't let that happen, but let's not take any chances."

As he talks, Larry opens a bottle of Liz's favorite Merlot, sniffs the open top to check the aroma and says, "This should be a great one, ladies. I think you know more about aging wine than you've let on, Liz."

"Oh, it's easy… I buy cases of excellent wine from upstart wineries and lay the wine boxes on their sides on the lowest shelf in the pantry. It's a perfect temperature for reds and that's all I buy. Then, once a month for five years, I turn the boxes over."

Mary hangs the dish towel on the oven's handle, then goes to sit in one of the two overstuffed chairs which face the stone fireplace. Looking at Larry pointing his hand at the front of the firebox, she asks, "Do you really think we need a fire tonight? It's still nearly seventy degrees outside."

Smiling at his wife, Larry says, "It's always necessary to have a fire in any fireplace, Mary. Especially, after a great dinner like Liz just served us. We can't sit in here and look at imaginary flames. Besides, this is a gas fireplace and I can light it with a flick of this remote. These things are more pretty then practical as they don't give off that much heat any time of the year."

When her husband sets the remote on the fireplace mantle, Mary takes a sip from the wine glass in front of her and feels a cool breeze wafting into the room through the open door to the deck. Startled, she scolds, "Larry, you left the slider door wide open. Weren't we going to lock up the house? There's only a screen door across that opening. That won't keep Dan from getting into Liz's home."

Settling into the chair across from Mary, Larry smiles at his wife and says, "Calm down, old girl, I've got my gun right here by my side. Liz told me long ago that her pistol is in the pantry and she's in there getting it ready right now. She'll tuck hers under the pillow at the far end of the sofa. So relax. Sit back and sip your wine. Enjoy some of that great cheese on a cracker with this terrific Merlot. Besides, the chances of Dan going over to the restaurant and getting back here by seven are slim to none. I doubt he'll stand us up, so it'll be a couple hours before he gets here. Besides, there's three of us and we have Kip on our side. So relax, kid, enjoy the last of a splendid meal neither of us had to cook."

Just then, Liz comes from the pantry and goes to the sofa. Immediately, the couple sees she is carrying an impressive pistol in her right hand. Setting it beside the tray of cheeses and wine glasses on the coffee table, Liz looks at the couple and smiles. "Yes, you are both right, it's Liz Oakley with her six shooter by her side."

Laughing, Larry asks, "Do you think it would be best if Mary and I hide in the pantry? Or do you want Dan to see us all together when he first gets here?"

"Stay with me. This has been a perfect evening, Larry. Let's not let the thought of him coming here spoil it. If he comes and that's a big if, he'll see us together and know we caught him in his duplicity. He may even leave without coming inside. I want to assure you both that I'm not as naïve as I may sound right now. I know how to use this pistol and I will use it if I have to do so. Right now, I'm tucking it here under the pillow on this end of the sofa."

"How can you be so calm, Liz." Mary asks as she spreads a cracker with the stinky cheese."

"I assure you, Mary, I'm on alert. I'm on hold and in my wait and watch mode. I don't believe Dan will do anything to me, but I'm very afraid he'll try to hurt Kip. He knows how important my darling dog is to me. That's what scares me, Mary, and why I must keep very calm."

Larry nods, 'I've been thinking a lot about Dan's invites to the three of us and that makes the most sense. Now, with the three of us here, he will at least have to adjust his plans those first few seconds and that may give us time to stall or stop whatever it is he wants to do here."

"I agree, Larry. The first and only being to protect tonight is Kip. In fact, Kip, come here and lay next to me. That's a good boy. Tuck yourself under the coffee table. Good. See how nicely you're hidden if Dan comes through the slider door."

"Liz is right, Mary. We don't really know if that guy means to harm to any of us. Let's just relax and enjoy the evening. When he realizes we're not showing up at the restaurant, he may go up to our house first before he comes down here. I think we should just enjoy the wine and sunset as usual."

Frowning, Liz says, "Oh, Dan will be here at seven as he promised me. He planned to leave the two of you sitting on the other side of Discovery Bay. I doubt if he ever intended to meet you there. He sent you there to get even with Mary asking him about the phone calls. When I showed Dr. Vale that broken bottle that cut Kip's paw, she agreed that it was buried very recently. The broken edge was new and we both could smell the whiskey."

"I still don't understand why anyone would make such a mess of his own life. Does he belong to any fringe groups that you know of, Liz?"

"Not that I know of, Mary. But, for some reason, my taking Kip to see Dr. Vale at his office, triggered something in Dan's mixed up head. Whatever trouble he wants to cause Kip and I comes from his sick mind. We're the ones on his hit list. I'm with Mary, Dan made those stupid phone calls and, I'm just as certain, he was the person who buried those pieces of that bottle in the sand. The idiot actually used an empty bottle from his favorite whiskey and it probably has his fingerprints all over it."

"But how would he be able to bury it so close to your house? Wouldn't Kip know he was out there?"

"I asked Kip about that and he said not from the north cliffs. Dan knew we run to the cliffs every morning and I often run bare footed this time of the year. The asshole intended that I would step on it, not Kip. When I told him how badly hurt Kip was, he was shocked. Yeah. The stupid jerk meant the glass for me."

Mary says, "I agree... I've never said it, but I've always felt that bottle was meant for you and Kip's stepping on it was a terrible mistake. Larry, I think it's time to show Liz what you brought with you tonight."

"Hell, Mary do you think that's necessary? I was going to until she brought out her own pistol. Besides, Liz knows I carry my pistol most of the time. However, I guess I should tell you both that I have a friend tailing Parker as we speak. The person is retired CIA and very good. Yes, Mary, it's him and he owed us a big favor for covering his butt last year."

Hearing this, Liz says, 'Holy cow, Larry, is there anything you can't do? You two are amazing. What else is there about you two that I don't know?"

Mary laughs, "Not tonight, kiddo. I see on your mantle clock that it's about to strike seven. By now, Dan must realize Larry and I aren't joining him for dinner or he may be here. Kip? Are you watching the door? Larry, talk to Liz so you can face us both. Kip will let Liz know when Dan's close by before he shows himself. Won't you, Kip?"

*Tell her I've heard every word and already planned to do what she said.*

Liz smiles and repeats Kip's words to Mary who smiles at the dog and says, "What a good boy you are, Kip."

At this time, Larry says, "At least we know he'll enter through the open slider door and the screen should give us a few seconds to react. If he's gone to the restaurant and been seated, he may wait to greet us before taking his leave. If so, this past half-hour has him getting very antsy about our not appearing."

When his cell phone rings, Larry answers with a short, "Talk to me."

The two women stare wide eyed as he listens for a few seconds then hangs up without commenting into the phone. "Dan's car is on Shoreline Drive and he'll be down your driveway in seconds. Mary? Why don't you go dish up that fruit torte you baked and I lugged over here. While you're doing that, I'll fill our wine glasses. We should be enjoying ourselves when Dan gets here. Okay with you, Liz?"

While the couple busies themselves, Liz leans back against the pillow on the sofa end and chats as the couple work along the kitchen counter. It's when Mary sets the dessert plates close to where they are seated, that Kip moves rapidly from under the coffee table and lays in front of the stone fireplace.

Alarmed, Liz starts to stand up and Kip's words shout in her head, *Sit down and stay down. Do not move. He is here. Eat your dessert. Now.*

Shocked, Liz stares at the dog without saying a word. However, Kip closes his eyes and heaves a great sigh, Mary laughs, "Mr. K, are you with us? Remember, we need your nose on alert for any scent of the boogieman."

Looking at Mary, Liz mouths, "He's here."

At that time, the mantle clock chimes seven and Kip's ears swivel towards the front of the house and move towards the open slider door. All three watch the animals feigned sleep and knows the dog's full attention is caught by something they can't see.

Laughing loudly, Larry slides his hand down to touch the cold metal of the pistol beside him. Leaning back against the pillows on the sofa, Liz kicks off her sandals and stretches her legs straight out towards the open door.

Turning towards the Jacksons, she says in a normal voice, "Hey, I want you both to know what great friends you've both been and tonight has been lovely. I'm so glad you moved into that house of yours."

Dropping her head towards the floor, Mary says quietly, "Kip sees something I don't. Where the hell is the S.O.B.?"

As if Mary's words are a command, Kip moves into a crouch and growls deep in his throat. All three people watch his reaction and know what is coming before Dr. Dan Parker kicks through the screen door and lunges into the cabin.

"Why are you two here? Larry? Mary? Didn't I tell you to meet me at the restaurant at seven o'clock? You shouldn't be here. I can't be responsible for what is going to happen to you. Don't you understand? These two are evil. Children of the devil. I have to rid the world of them and the burn down this house to be rid of their evil. Liz and Kip are not of our world and I am charged with getting rid of them. I must save the world from their evil." Dan Parker screams as he stands at the end of the dining table waving a large pistol in each of his hands.

Glaring at the man, Liz shouts, "Shut up, Parker, and get the fuck out of my house. I told you that you're not welcome here. Not ever. So get out. Now."

Her intense anger surprises the man and he stays next to the dining table over the golden stone in the floor with a puzzled expression across his face. For several seconds, the man simply stares at the three people in front of him as if not knowing what to do next. However, when he sees Kip crouched in front of the fireplace, his face changes and his aims both guns at the dog.

In that instant, the golden stone fills the room with light so brilliant that all the humans have to close their eyes or be blinded. Screaming, Parker drops one of the pistols on the table to cover his eyes with his free hand. At that same moment, Kip leaps across the room and lands upon the man's chest, knocking him down on the polished cement floor and bites down hard on the hand holding the gun.

As the animal's teeth sink into his flesh, Parker screams in pain and rolls back and forth, shooting wildly three times. Then the gun goes off twice more and those bullets ricochet off the stone fireplace and one zings past Liz's head which makes her furious.

"You stupid bastard, you nearly shot me in the head. I told you to get out of here. Go away and never come back. What the hell did you think you would do by coming here tonight? I'm calling the police."

As she yells, both Larry and Mary rush over to where Kip is holding Parker where he fell on the floor by the dining table. Every time the man struggles to get up off the floor, the dog bites harder and Parker screeches with pain. Sitting on top of the man, Larry pulls the man's arms behind his back and Marry ties them with the cord from the kitchen phone. Then Larry ties Parker's feet together by using the laces of the man's shoes.

Turning Parker over, Larry pulls Dan into a sitting position and sets him against the back of the chair by the fireplace. It's then, that Dan Parker begins to jerk his body up and down trying to get onto his feet and yells, "Damn you both. Let me go. Why are you helping her? You were supposed to meet me at that restaurant on the other side of the bay. Help me. Kill these evil beings. Damn, you. Don't you hear me? Untie me. I command you to untie me or take my pistol and kill them both. Get away from me, Kip. Let go of my hand. Larry, make the damn dog let go of my hand. Mary? Help me. Tell Larry to make Kip let go of me."

Walking away from Dan as he struggles with Kip and Larry, Mary carries Dan's two pistols by the barrels and set them into the kitchen sink and sees Liz is talking into her cellphone.

"Yes, sir. Mr. Jackson has bound Dan Parker's hands and feet. Please hurry. Yes, we will. No, we're sure his hands and feet are secured. Yes, I will. Thank you. We'll make certain he doesn't go anywhere."

As she ends the call, Kip releases the man's bloody hand and moves close to where Liz is standing by the kitchen counter. Looking down at the bedraggled man, Liz says, "Shit, Dan, you sure know how to screw up your life, don't you?"

It's then that Larry lifts Parker onto his feet, turns him slightly and pushes him down into one of the dining chairs at the table. For several minutes, Dan sits silent with his head hanging down and weeping openly. "I've failed my mission. Please, dear Lord, forgive me, I know this was not what we planned I was to do. I tried my best and failed you. I'm sorry, dear Lord. I'm sorry. Please forgive me."

Then, the seemingly pitiful man weeps loudly until Larry takes the dish towel off the oven handle and wipes Dan's face. Waiting until he blows his nose, Larry looks at the two women and shakes his head. It's then that Liz turns her attention to Kip and sees the dog is covered with blood from biting on Dan's wrist.

Hurrying to the kitchen, Liz pours water in a bowl and calls Kip over to be washed. Wiping the mess off the animal's snout and fur, they are where Parker can see them and he becomes inflamed with renewed energy. Standing up off the chair, he twists his body towards Liz and throws himself forward trying to butt her with his head.

Instantly, Kip lunges at the man, grabs between his legs and spins under the man. The force of Kips movement throws Parker off balance and he turns on his shoes tied together by their laces. At first, it looks as if he was simply returning to the chair, then he bends over screaming from the pain of the dog holding onto his genitals.

At the same time, Larry grabs the man by one arm and tries to push him down onto the dining chair. Instead of sitting, though, Dan Parker pulls back and twists hard to the right, freeing himself from Larry's grip. The force of his moves causes Dan to lose his balance and fall headfirst toward the sharp corner of the dining table.

Watching helplessly, the other three hear the man's head hit the corner with a loud crack and, with that sound, see Dr. Dan Parker drops heavily to the floor, his legs splayed towards the open slider door. First there is a gush of blood, then grey matter spills from the opening in his forehead and lays on the polished cement floor near Liz's dining table.

Even though she was furious at the man, Liz is instantly sickened by the sound and turns away retching. Only Mary Jacksons goes to kneel beside Parker's still body and touches the man's neck to feel for a pulse. When she looks up at Larry, she shakes her head, but Liz already knows that Dr. Dan Parker is gone.

Going over to the sofa, Liz takes her cell phone off the coffee table and sits down, then she calls 911 and tells them to send an ambulance with the response team. Hearing her words, the Jacksons quickly join her in front of the fireplace and Mary says, "I don't really understand why he thought you and Kip were so evil. Why would he want to kill you? What was it just a stupid game he was playing? Why ask us out to dinner and coming here with a pistol instead? I'd think a box of candy and flowers would have worked better if all he wanted was to turn you back from whatever evil he thought was in you."

"I have no answers, Mary. I never heard him voice any concerns about either me or Kip last year before I told who and what we are. Then he left without a word to anyone. At least the way it is now, he'll never threaten anyone again."

Turning away, Liz pulls her gun from under the sofa cushion and says to Larry, "Bring your gun and come with me."

Then she leads Larry him into the pantry and closes the door behind them. Taking his gun from him, she places it and her own pistol into the open safe in the sidewall. Then, Liz closes the safe's door and spins the dial three times.

When they walk back to where Mary and Kip are waiting, both glance at the body blocking the open slider door. Sitting again on the far end of the sofa, Kip comes to her and lays down next to her feet. As he heaves a big sigh, Liz hears.

*I've had enough excitement. Good night.*

Stroking the dog, Liz looks at each of her friends now sitting in the chairs on either side of the fireplace and says, "Thank you both so much. Thank God, you were here when Dan arrived. I shudder to think of what might have happened if I had been alone. I truly never dreamed that he was capable of anything so terrible."

"No, neither did I," Larry says, "It seems Dr. Dan Parker was a very sick man. When we first met him, he told of how hard it was to make new friends in Ocean Shores. Now, I'm not surprised, if he judged everyone as harshly as he did you and Kip. The only reason his veterinarian business could have thrived was that he kept his thoughts to himself during those hours. When Mary and I took those injured seals to him last year, he seemed a caring sort of person and quite charming. He had those seals back to health in a few weeks and didn't charge us anything. Both Mary and I were thrilled to find such a generous good man living in our new community."

"There... aren't those sirens in the distance? The County Sheriff or ambulance is on its way. Probably both. Let's discuss what we should say about what happened." Mary says.

Liz says, "No discussion is necessary, Mary. Just tell it like it happened in your own words. We finished our meal, did the dishes and were enjoying dessert when Dan opened the screen door, rushed inside and began shooting. Kip leapt at him, grabbed the hand with the pistol and Larry rushed to help. When he had Dan secured, I commanded Kip to let go of Parker's hand. Larry helped Dan to his feet and placed him in that chair. You picked up his two guns and placed them in the kitchen sink. Several minutes later, Dan staggered to his feet and tried to get away. Evidently, he didn't realize his shoes were tied together and twisted around until he fell forwards hitting his head on the corner of the table."

Mary replies, "Of course, that's exactly what I saw. However, do we need to tell about Dan's dinner invitations or his calls to us before hand? What do you think?"

Larry nodded, "Of course not, Mary. Remember the K.I.S.S. of your training, my girl. Keep it simple, stupid. Only tell it as it happened when Dan got here. They'll want to know why Dan came here with a gun. Liz will have to tell them of their involvement last year and how he tried to get back with her and that she wouldn't. That he came through the slider door with both pistol firing and how Kip was the evening's hero. I was completely surprised by how often Dan shot at us. If Kip hadn't grabbed his hand and held on, I doubt I could have tied him up. Without Kip, Dan would have done as he planned and there'd be three or more bodies in this room."

Mary nods, "Yes, you are so right. Only after tying his hands and feet together were you able to set him into that chair and let go of him. When he began sobbing, he seemed so subdued that I dropped my guard. I was shocked when he got to his feet and fell forward hitting his head on that corner of the table. It all happened in seconds."

"No need to talk about the brilliant light that stopped Dan and gave Kip a chance to leap onto him. Even we don't understand how that happened. Just say the truth in your own words. They'll interview each of us separately to see how our stories vary, so add things about the dinner and doing dishes, whatever comes to you. Leave out the before and unexplained light." Larry tells his wife. Then to assure her, he goes over and gives her a warm hug and quick kiss.

Liz nods, "Thank God the golden stone reacted. Was that you, Kip?"
*Dan needed to be stopped. Now stop talking. The Sheriff is here.*

# FIVE

## June 5<sup>th</sup>—Beth

**BETH** walks through the deck's slider door just as the front door is thrown open with a slam and her niece Nicole pushes her way into the cabin carrying a suitcase in each hand. Not seeing Beth, the young woman takes them straight into the bedroom directly across from the front door. When she comes back into the room, she sees her Aunt and shouts, "Hey, Aunt Beth, I didn't see you there. Sorry I made such a racket. I'm here for the summer with everything I own, is that okay?"

Whooping, "Yahoo!" Beth rushes across the room to grab Nicole into a bear hug and yelps, "I'll say it is. What a wonderful surprise. Welcome home, darling girl. How'd your finals go?"

"I got a B plus on my orals to finalize my doctorate. Pretty grand, huh? Since that's finished, I was kicked out of my grad-student apartment and had to downsize to an affordable studio off campus. I signed the lease yesterday but it won't be available until late August. So I decided to come out here and stay with you. I'm so glad you like the idea."

Beth laughs and hugs her again, saying, "I'm delighted. Do you need help bringing in anything else?"

"Sure do." Nicole answers as she goes back out the front door with Beth right behind her.

After two more trips to the back of Nicole's Subaru Forester, Nicole's possessions are piled inside the bedroom. Standing in the doorway of the room, both Aunt and Niece stare at the boxes piled on the bed and suitcases pushed against the walls of the small room. It's Beth who first begins to chuckle and soon is roaring with laughter as she slides down the doorjamb to sit on the floor.

Dropping down beside her, Nicole says, "I know, I know... I should have dumped more of this stuff in the trash cans on campus. But honestly, I thought that thrift shop in Ocean Shores might want most of my discards. Those four boxes will go back out to my Forester and I'll take them there later. There'll probably more stuff as I unpack. Right now, though, I'm starving and would love some breakfast. After that I'll haul those boxes down to that shop. When I get back I'll settle into my room. I promise. Does that sound sane enough for you?"

"Everything you say sounds sane enough to me, darling girl. Especially about being starved and needing breakfast. Let's go fix it. You make the coffee and I'll start the bacon. I've discovered a great way to microwave it so that it's nearly fat free and very crispy, just as you like it. Sound okay?"

"Yummy!" Nicole exclaims and pushes her aunt out to the kitchen stove. As she fixes the coffee maker, the two women chat and the cabin fills with the wonderful aromas of the coming breakfast. Soon both are sitting at the dining table and enjoying their first summer breakfast together.

Beth says, "It's going to be great having you here for the whole summer. If you signed that lease on a studio off campus, you must have plans to work in Seattle this fall. Where?"

"Gosh, I forgot to tell you about the job I'm to start this fall. Guess I was too excited about being out here with you. I applied to three postings as soon as I was sure of getting my PhD. It's very competitive in my field and housing close to campus would be gone by fall. That's why I signed the lease so early. Anyway, I applied for the positions as soon as they were announced and called to interview for all of them. I accepted the one I wanted most, half day teaching and half day research. It starts end of August and should fast track to a permanent position in that department. I'll be working directly under my mentor, Professor Patricia Miles. She's highly regarded in her field worldwide and I'm thrilled to be able to work with her."

"That's marvelous, Nicole. I remember Patricia. She was in several classes with me when I was at the U and a child prodigy if I remember correctly. I'm happy to hear she's done so well. What plans do you have for your time here? Just R and R?"

"No, not at all. I'm going to work for Lucy Wong, your neighbor up the road. I'll be collecting samples off the south beach cliffs. I start Monday. I'll give her a call later. I saw there's a cell tower on that high point off the south curve on Shoreline Drive. I tried my phone as soon as I got here and it was good. How does it feel to be in the twenty-first century?"

"Absolutely wonderful. I got a smart phone the minute I heard they were building that tower and even got a computer. Now I'm on the internet and have a TV to stream off the internet. Look over the fireplace. Everything's up to date on my lonely Redcliff's Beach cabin. When I started using the smart phone, I was dazzled by all the things that can do. I tell you, Nicole, that internet's like going back to University. I already have a couple hundred old friends catching up on face book. People who were in Maxine's and my lives years ago. I must say I enjoy reading what they're doing."

"Word of warning, Aunt Beth, you can get pulled into that thing and become its slave. Take care not to give away all your secrets to everybody who asks."

"I've already figured that out. Some of the things people say are so shocking. I've decided not to answer those. The internet seems like a good way to get yourself into deep trouble or to offend everyone you know in one fell swoop."

Smiling at her Aunt, Nicole says, "That's very wise of you, darling. I'm careful about what I write on social sites as everything you do stays there forever. I've friends who sent nude photos to men friends when they were younger and now regret it... Today, employers expect to be able to look at any applicant's Facebook postings and Tweets. It's part of every job interview."

"Then I was right not to get started. No telling what stupid things I'd have written by now." Beth chuckles.

"Nah, you're way too smart to do that, Aunt Beth. How's your darling Ann doing? I hope she'll come through later today. It's been a while since I've seen her."

"She's doing great. Her small cabin on her basalt point is finished and quite wonderful. It's tiny but very comfortable. If she's out there, she might come through to us as we're sitting here right now. Her dog, Honey, often sleeps with Dandy on the golden stone. Kip too. Those animals get together more often than the three of us do. I'm glad you asked about Ann. I couldn't remember if I'd told you about my love for her. But, calling her 'my darling Ann', tells me I did. We are going to make it official late this summer. In fact, I'll make sure we do it before you go back to Seattle."

"That'd be great, Aunt Beth. I'm so happy for you both. How's it work with being in different dimensions?"

"Actually, it seems our dimensions agree with our decision. Any time we want to be together, we're zapped into the other's dimension. We're hardly ever apart. I simply lay my hands on this golden agate bowl that came off the south cliffs or slap the touchstone at the north cliffs and we're together."

"I'd love to help you on the day."

"We will say our vows at the north cliffs. Ann asked her sister, Dana, to stand up with her and I was going to ask if you'd be with me."

"Oh Aunt Beth, I'd love to be with you at your wedding ceremony. When it's my turn, you will you return the favor. Is it a deal?"

"It's a deal. Liz will come with Kip. Ann will bring Honey and Dandy will come with us. Dandelion now goes with me on my runs. She likes to hide in the drift logs along the beach. I love that kitty of yours so much, I may never give her back to you when you have you own place."

"Oh, don't worry about that, Aunt Beth, Dandy gave me the heave-ho the minute she saw the beach. Dandy belongs to you and only you. How is she with Ann and Honey? As I remember, that sweet looking cat can be fiercely protective toward someone she doesn't like. Where is she now?"

"Thanks for reminding me. The last time I saw her, she was snagging tidbits out of Lucy's specimen discard bucket. Would you like to run up the touchstone and say Hi to Lucy? We might go through to Ann's dimension and maybe Liz will be there too. It's amazing how often the three of us spend mornings at Ann's cliff top kitchen. Why don't we go now? I'll help you take your boxes into Ocean Shores later this afternoon."

"OH, yes, Aunt Beth, I'd love it if I go through to Ann's. I've wanted to see that crystal room. It sounds so wonderful."

"You'll be wowed... I just remembered something Ann told me yesterday, her sister, Dana, has moved up from Los Angeles and Ann wants to give Dana half of the house and the land. She says their parents would have wanted them to be together at this time of their lives. If we go into the crystal cave or Ann's dimension, we might meet her, also."

"Gosh, Aunt Beth, that would be so exciting. Do you think she would like to meet me? Isn't Dana my mother's Parallel Life? Does she look much like my Mom?"

"Oh, yes, dear girl. Startlingly so. Her looks are Dee's in every way. Only her personality is the direct opposite of what your mother's was. Dana's joyful person and shows her art work all around the world. Now that she moved up here two years ago, she runs a sales gallery in Ocean Shore. She's quite a famous artist in their dimension. If we go into the crystal room today and Dana's with Ann, try not to be too shocked. Just remember, she is not your mother. Do you still want to give it a try?"

"Oh, yes, Aunt Beth, I'd love to meet Dana. If I'm don't go through with you, will you tell her about me? Maybe she'll come through at the adjoined tables. Look, Aunt Beth, see how the agate bowl glows when I touch it? Do you think that's a good sign?"

"Yes, dear. It's a wonderful sign. I'm so glad for you. It may be that you essence has replaced Dee's in this dimension. Let's get going. I can't wait to see Ann and have Dana meet you."

"Let's go. I'm going to think of nothing else all the way to the cliffs."

"That's how I do it. Good for you for thinking that way. Come on, I really want to see what happens at the touchstone."

When they reach the granite slab, the two women hurry over to stand in front of the stone glowing in the cliff face. However, as they raise their hands to slap the golden stone, a horn honks several times and they turn to see Lucy Wong's pickup pulling up in front of the Airstream trailer parked at the end of the roundabout on Shoreline Drive. When they wave, Lucy shouts, "Come up for tea when you're done."

Waving back, Beth tells Nicole, "You can go join Lucy if you'd rather. We can always try for the crystal room tomorrow."

"No siree, I'm slapping the touchstone with you and let it make that decision for me." Nicole says taking hold of her Aunt Beth's hand. Then the two women slap the stone at the same time and shout, "I declare this run good and done."

Instantly, the pair find themselves in the center of the large open cave covered with thousands upon thousands of crystal formations of various sizes and colors. Still holding her Aunt's hand, Nicole gasps, "My gosh. Aunt Beth, we're in the crystal room. How beautiful. Even though you told me it was amazing, I never really understood what your amazing meant. This room has to be the most beautiful place in the whole world. Thank you for bringing me here. Lordy, I never want to leave. Can I walk around and look everywhere? This is the most glorious place I've ever seen. I feel as if I've come into God's house. It's more holy that any of those huge cathedrals they built all over Europe."

"Glad you like it, my darling Nicole. Now breathe deeply and go look around the room. Take your time. Snoop everywhere. See that bench along the far left of the room? See how it attaches to those crystal thrones? That's where we last saw Eliza and your mother during last year's Summer Solstice. Eliza's essence came here after she was killed by your mother. When she came to us, we felt her words instead of heard them. She wanted to say goodbye to us, her Parallel Lives. We felt a loving warmth from her essence. From Dee's essence we only felt cold around her. Nothing else."

"Eliza told us the large white dog was called Karma. It stood between her essence and Dee's. I'm not sure if Karma was his name or if he was the phenomenon known as Karma. Anyway, Eliza followed him when James and Jill Anderson said it was time to go down the stairs into the wormhole opening below that crystal throne. Dee followed at a distance, but before her parents, James and Jill Anderson."

As Beth tells her these things, Nicole walks over to touch the crystal groupings closest to her. Then, she moves to the center of the fire-opal tiles and begins to turn around in one spot. After doing this several times around, Nicole stops and stares across the room and hears Beth shout, "Hi darling, I was hoping you'd come here this morning."

Startled by the words, Nicole turns just as Beth crosses the room to stop next to two backlit women who are at the bottom of the stairs that come from the opening in the roof of the cave. Squinting against the bright light, Nicole sees Beth talking to the shadowed faces and hurrying over to her Aunt, saying, "Aunt Beth, who are you talking to? Is it Ann? I can't see them against the sunlight from that hole in the ceiling. Aunt Beth?"

As she moves, the light goes behind her and Nicole sees the women's face and she cries out, "Mommy? Mommy, is that you/ Ae you really here?"

Instantly, Beth steps in front of her niece and pulls her into her arms, saying, "No, Nicole, this is Dana Anderson, Ann's sister. She's not your mother. Remember, I told you we would see Ann and her sister? You remember Ann, don't you? The woman next to her is Dana, her sister. She is your mother Dee's Parallel Life. Though she looks exactly like your mother did, she is not Dee. Stand here with me and calm yourself. When you're ready, I'll introduce you to Dana. All right?"

Nodding, Nicole holds her Aunt in tight hug and takes several deep quivering breaths. When she is calm, Nicole slowly turns and looks at Dana's face and her eyes fill with tears and says, "Hello, Dana, I want to apologize for my outburst. There for a moment, I thought you were my mother... Dee... that she had come back. Of course, you're not her. Aunt Beth warned me before we came here that you'd look exactly like her. Still it was such a shock to see how you look exactly like her. I'm Nicole McGowan and my Mom was one of your Parallel Lives, Dee McGowan. I'm one of her twin daughters. My sister Nancy lives back East."

As Nicole speaks, Dana places her hands on Nicole's shoulders and says, "It's lovely to meet you, Nicole. I know what a shock it must have been to see me, as I was shocked to see you. You are exactly as my twin daughters would have looked at your age. My twins, Janice and Jill, died in a head-on car crash two years ago, the night of their college graduation."

Watching the two meet each other, brings tears to Beth eyes and she says, "I forgot about your children, Dana. I should have told Nicole about them. Are you two going to be okay around each other?"

"Yes, Beth. I came down the stairs and when I saw Nicole standing in the middle of the room I thought she was one of my own. Thank God, you and Ann were with us. I didn't know Nicole would be here today. Luckily, Ann heard me gasp and grabbed hold of my arm to hold me here. Even so, as you walked over to us, all I saw was one of my own twins. I'm so sorry, Nicole, I'm not able to be so close without touching you. I guess it's going to take time for us to get used to each other. Would you mind if I wrapped my arms around you for a short while?"

"I would love that, Dana, please do. Don't be shocked if I call you Mom and I won't be shocked if you call me Jill or Janice. I'm sorry they were taken from you. I would have loved to have known them."

As the two women hold onto each other, a soft wind wafts into the crystal room and swirls around the four women, caressing the crystals. Soon, the cave is filled with wondrous soft chiming that calm women as memories of what might have been fill their heads.

When Dana and Nicole part, each smiles at the other and Dana says, "I can't begin to tell you how wonderful it is for me to know that somewhere in the Universe there are Parallel Lives exactly like my twins who are living happy healthy lives. Thank you so much, Nicole.

Feeling you next to me has given me a sense of relief I've not felt since their deaths. Thank you so much, darling Nicole."

Unable to answer, Nicole only nods and hugs the woman again. This time when they part, Ann says, "Ladies, I think it would be best if we go out to the cliff tops and enjoy the sunshine. I left the picnic basket on the table with Honey standing guard. Even though I gave her a new knuckle bone to gnaw on, I might have left the fox to guard the henhouse. Let's hope she's still guarding and not enjoying our food.

Beth hugs Ann and says, "Great idea, sweetheart. Let's go get comfy, eat your lovely lunch and have a long chat. The morning news said my dimension was to expect a big storm late tonight. Times like these, I wish my cabin was on a high hill as Ann's house is."

Nicole agrees, "Yes, I'm ready to get out of here. This flashing light off the crystals is killing my eyes, even with my wraparound sunglasses."

As the women walk down to the cliff top kitchen, Dana says, "Looks as if your luck held, Ann. The basket is untouched and Honey is still chewing her knuckle bone."

Once the lunch is spread out on the table, the four women take their filled plates and settle along the benches. Leaning back against the sun heated stacked stone wall, the four silently munch the delicious food and watch huge rolling waves crash onto the rocky shore.

Finally, Beth says, "I've never been here when there was a storm. Those waves get higher with each swell. It certainly makes me appreciate this windbreak Ann built here years ago."

"I don't know if Ann ever told you, Beth, but when I used to visit her, I never came down to the beach. It's such a perfect a view her deck, there never seemed a good reason to come down here. Also, the Redcliff's Beach I knew as a kid was gone. This new one seemed to belong to Ann. However, that changed last Christmas, when Ann insisted I come down to the clifftops with her. We sat here next to the wall and she built a fire in the fireplace. Then she told me how she'd found the crystal room when she was a young child and took me down to see it. I was awed. It was the most perfect Christmas present I'd ever received."

Turning to her sister, Dana continues, "I lived here every summer during my childhood just as you did, Ann, and I was never curious about these cliffs. I never dreamed a cave of any sort existed. I don't understand how I could have had so little curiosity about what you loved on these clifftops. Wasn't I pathetic?"

Chuckling, Ann says, "No, Dana, not pathetic. You were just a little girl with other interests. When I built the kitchen, you decided it was something I needed to do and you've respected this place as my personal space."

"It was generous of Ann to finally invite you into the crystal room. Liz and I had to find it on our own. I remember the first time Ann saw us down there, I could see that she didn't like our being there, not one bit. I'm right, aren't I, Ann? You didn't want to share the crystal cave you'd sheltered from the world."

Tucking her head, Ann looks at Beth and says, "Yes, I admit it did at first. This whole cliff top and crystal room had been mine for my whole life. It was only on the Summer Solstice last year, when I saw James and Jill Anderson disappear into the wormhole with Eliza's white dog herding Eliza and Dee's essences ahead of it that I realized the crystal room didn't belong to me. It was never mine. It belongs to the Universe. I've only been a caretaker. It's our parents, James and Jill Anderson, who are charged with its care. All the Elizabeth Ann Andersons, our Parallel Lives, and their families, no matter who are the future caretakers of that cave."

Nicole says, "Gosh, Ann, I'm so glad you've come to feel that way. I wondered if it was okay to come with Aunt Beth today. She assured me that it was."

"It's more than alright, Nicole, it's wonderful that you came today. You and your generation are the future caretakers. In fact, I want to thank Beth for bringing you with her this morning. It's was a joy to watch you and Dana meet each other and I welcome you with all my heart. As you can see, my dimension is very different than Beth's and Liz's. I wonder if there is anything you'd especially like to see on this first visit?"

"Oh, yes, please. Could we hike down to your cabin on the far point?

Beth's told me so much about what you've done down there. I'd love to see the golden stone in the cement floor for myself. Dandelion always sleeps there in Beth's cabin and both Honey and Kip were both with her on the stone when we left for our run."

Dana stands, "What a great idea, Nicole. I've been down there several times since Ann first took me to it. You are right when you say it's a very special place. I love being near that stone again. As a child, I played all over it. That stone is the most direct tie to my mother and father, Jill and James Anderson, your grandparents..."

Beaming at her family, Ann says, "What a great idea. Let's do it. I love showing off my handy work and it would be the perfect thing to do on this windy day. Come along, Honey. Lead us down the trail to the cabin and we'll sit around the table over Dad's golden stone."

Reaching the bridge at the end of the basalt flow, the four women comment on the lengths of driftwood Ann used to reach across the low sea stacks. As she moves over to the cabin, Ann relates how she made each sturdy bridge to tie into the next, "You can thank Beth for all of it. If she hadn't asked about the golden stone being in the flat cement she saw on that larger sea stack I may never have thought to look for it. It's then that the two of us came down the beach, climbed the sea stack and found the stone. It was covered with driftwood, seaweed and barnacles. We cleared off what we could at that time to make sure it was what we'd hoped. It was so exciting to see the stone still intact and glowing under all that debris. I spent days scrapping the surface until it shone as it had before."

"I was thrilled for you when we found the stone. Mostly because it would be your connection to the rest of us. However, the idea of connecting each sea stack with these beautiful driftwood float logs was your idea."

"Well, it was only way to get the bridges built as quickly as possible. Once they were done, I saw immediately that a small cabin was necessary to protect the table and chair over the golden stone. It was the only way I come down here daily and be certain to connect with you others at your adjoined tables. Now, enough, let's get into the cabin."

Without answering, the other three women follow her across the bridges and up to the front door. As they wait at the front door of the small building, Ann slips around to the south side of the cabin, fiddles with something along the wall and returns with a key to unlock the door. Opening it wide, she bows and says, "Welcome to my wee abode, my darling family."

Stepping inside, Nicole sees Honey is already lying beside the golden stone in the floor under the dining table and next to her are Kip and Dandy. Surprised by the animals, she says, "How the heck did those animals get in here so fast?"

Laughing, Ann says, "There's a dog door where I hide the key, so once it's open Honey comes inside. Her presence brings the other familiars, if they're beside their own stones. Maybe with Kip here, Liz will show up soon."

Turning to look at the cozy space, Ann says, "Oh, Ann, your cabin is wonderful. I see it's much smaller than Beth's cabin, but it's so well done, I don't miss what isn't here. Did you do this by yourself? Do you ever stay here?"

"I stay as often as possible as Beth and I are trying to make as much time for ourselves as possible. As for doing it myself, I built the framework and bolted everything into the cement floor. The metal roof and fireplace were done by a great contractor. I did the finishing myself, both inside and out. It's still such a joy to see how every little thing came together to make it mine."

As soon as she says this, Ann sees a sad look on Dana's face that she's not seen for a long while. Reaching over to hug her sister, Ann says, "However, now that Dana comes here, I realize she should have somethings in here as well. How would you like to do something to that bare wall? I've been stumped as to what should go there and maybe this is why. Do whatever you want to make you feel the cabin belongs as much to you as it does to me. Mom and Dad would want us to share the golden stone. Would you like to do something in here?"

"I'm not sure. This place seems so perfect now. Does it really need my touch? After all, Ann, you are the one who paid the taxes on Dad's land and who bought the land to the north and east. After all, you dedicated yourself to creating the kitchen on the cliffs, and built your house on the hillside years before I even returned for a visit. Remember, my darling sister, I was wrapped up in building my place in the art world. It's you who built this amazing cabin."

"Oh, Dana, don't you realize by now that I'm thrilled to have you come back to Redcliff's Beach and have you here close to me? I bless every day you come out here."

"Thank you, darling, your joy is my joy. Don't you feel how alive this cabin seems? I don't know how I could improve upon it. I will give your idea about the wall much thought. However, before I do anything, I will run it past you for an honest yea or nay. Is that clear?"

"That's clear. When I saw the sadness on your face, I felt badly that I'd never included you in any of the things you say make it so much mine."

"Trust me when I say this, Ann, The sadness I may have had on my face was that I never gave this place another thought after that storm swept away Dad's original cabin. That storm freed me and I gladly left it all to you. It's only now that I realize that I should have cared more than I did."

"I stayed because I knew what was inside those cliffs and I wasn't about to give it up to anyone outside our family. I'm so glad you aren't hurt by what I've done without your input. I'm also glad you loved the golden stone as a child as much as I did."

Suddenly, Honey barks loudly and the animals rush out through the pet door. Startled by their quick exit, Ann looks at the table and shouts, "Hey, Liz is here."

Shouting from her chair at the end of the table, Liz says, "Hi everyone. I'm so glad you're all here. Ann, Beth, Nicole and..? Holy cow, is that Dee? What the hell is she...? No, of course, you can't be Dee.

You must be Ann's sister, Dana. Right? Hi Dana, I'm Liz Day. Kip's my master and I meant that the way I said it."

Laughing with her, Dana says, "Nice to meet you, Liz. Though we haven't met before, I've heard so much about you and Kip that I feel as if I've known you both forever.""

Smiling at the exuberant woman, Nicole says, "It's great to see you again, Liz. I saw Kip at Aunt Beth's so figured we'd meet sometime today. Kip's quite a dog, isn't he?"

Grinning at her, Liz says, "I'll say he is. It's great that he has Honey and Dandy who accept him for what he is. Listen to our beasts enjoying themselves out there. I love that they're so good together. Sounds like they're having fun, doesn't it?"

"It sure does," Beth laughs, "It's so lovely that both dogs include Dandy-lion. I wonder if she ever shows them what a beast she actually is."

"Yes, she does. Kip told me. She turns into the tiger she is whenever the dogs get too rough with her. But, enough about them, I want to update you about what happened when I went into Neil Gardner's dimension this morning. Do you have time to listen?"

When the four women shout, 'Yes.' Liz begins telling what happened when she went into Neil's dimension and met with the young man An hour later, she finishes and the other women begin to speak all at once. Holding up one hand, she says, "Please. One question at a time, please."

"Is he still alone?" Beth asks.

"Not anymore. Several battalions of armed services are camped down there and the families who own the home are beginning to trickle back to their home. Mostly, he wanted you and Beth to know that he didn't mean to shoot you. Said he was so excited that he dropped the rifle or pulled the trigger when he only meant to use the scope. He is very sorry he hurt you both and very happy his aim was so bad."

Turning to her sister, Dana shouts, "What? Ann? You were shot? Why didn't you tell me about that?"

Ann shakes her head, "I simply forgot about it by the time you got back from your trip to down to LA to open that gallery show. It happened last week and the wound has healed. Most of the scab sluffed off in the shower this morning. I'll show you what's left when we get home. You're such a worrywart, Dana. It was only a flesh wound. Really."

Nicole starts to chuckle. When the women turn to her, Beth asks, "What's so funny, kiddo?"

Smiling at the three Parallel Lives of Elizabeth Ann and the one Parallel Life of Dee McGowan, Nicole says, "You sound just like my sister and me. Does every generation repeat these little fusses? If so, how do we ever become our own generation?"

"It just happens. You hold onto some things and reject others to form your own ideas and thoughts about life. What happens changes what will happen." Her Aunt answers. "How about it, Ann? Didn't you and Dana have a lot of squabbles?"

Dana shakes her head and says, "Nope. Ann and I didn't have squabbles. What we had open warfare."

The laughter that followed was so loud that it brought the three animals running back through the pet door. In that moment, Beth and Nicole and Dandy are back on their own granite slab on their own Redcliff's Beach and in their own dimension. Giving a quick meow, Dandelion crouches low, then streaks across the slab of rock, leaps onto the narrow strip of sand and runs a zig zag path towards the rip-rap edging Shoreline Drive's roundabout.

Looking at her aunt, Nicole shakes her head and says, "How do you stand this, Aunt Beth? I don't think I'll ever get used to popping in and out of different dimensions. Thank God, I don't do it often. Doesn't it drive you nuts?"

"Only once in a while and this is one of them. We were having such a good laugh over how we were and are now. It seems the Universe can't stand to see happy Elizabeth Anns get together. It's as if we were having too much fun, and the Universal Counsel says, 'Oh dear, better send them back to where they come from.' That's how it seems to me and, yes, it makes me crazy at times."

"Good. That shows me how normal you really are and I love you for it." Nicole tells her. "Why don't we go up to Lucy's for a while? I see her truck it there."

"You go, dear. Tell her Hi for me. I need to get downtown and do some shopping. Would you like me to take those boxes on the bed to the thrift shop?"

"That would be great, Aunt Beth. Just the three marked 'toss'. I'll go through the others this evening. How about I invite Lucy for dinner?"

"Of course. Please do."

# SIX

## *June 5th—Ann*

**ANN** is not at all surprised by the sudden disappearance of the others. However, Dana is completely undone and shouts, "What the… Damn, Ann, I don't think I'll ever get used to these comings and goings that you Parallel Lives do. No matter how often I see it happen, it shocks me. I don't see how you can do it without making you a bit odd."

Grinning at her sister, Ann says, "So who says I'm not a bit odd? Aren't we all or are you too odd to notice?"

"Oh hush. It's time to we go back the house before that wind wraps the waves up around the cabin and we have to stay overnight. I have the definite need to have several unchangeable moments. Though I say that, Ann, please know that I was thrilled to meet Nicole today. She was so like both of my girls."

"Yes, I could see how emotional you got. Losing a child must horrible and losing two must have nearly driven you insane."

"Their deaths certainly drove a wedge between their father and me. If I hadn't had my art to turn to I may have committed suicide just as he did. It was lovely meeting both Nicole and Beth. I'm sorry they left. Still, it is nice being here and having you and Honey all to myself."

"And I like being with you, my darling sister." Ann says. "Honey and I want you to visit us as often as you want and come down to the cabin whenever you like, with or without my being here. Come on, I'll show you where I leave the key. Then we'll go up to the house and get dinner in the oven. Remind me to pick up the picnic basket where I left it beside the trail."

"Okay. I think I'll eat the other half of my sandwich then. That half I had for lunch was not nearly enough for this old gal,"

"Come, Honey. Time we go home." Ann calls as she heads towards the door.

Bounding up from the golden stone, Honey gives an excited woof and runs out through the pet door. Ann laughs, "Guess she's ready to go home, too. Come on, I'll show you where the key goes."

After closing and locking the door, Ann walks to the south side of the cabin and stops beside the pet door. Pointing down at it, she says, "See that hook set on the one side of the pet door? That's where I hang the key. Then, I close this pocket door over the flap like this and flip these two black metal clips down into place. Voila, the pet door totally disappears. Unless you know to lift those solid looking clips, you wouldn't know the dog door was there."

"Wow, Ann. That's really neat. Can I try it?"

"Sure. See if you can flip the clips up. Good. Now slide that door out of the way. Voila… there's the key. Now you are in on the secret of getting into the cabin anytime you want, without me. If you forget to put the key back, don't worry. I have extras up at the house and I'll show you where I hang those."

"Thanks, Ann, I'd have never found that door by myself. It's a great way to hide both the key and the pet door. Now I'll come down to the cabin when you're busy with other things. Which makes me ask, are you planning any trips this summer?"

"Only to my class reunion in August. Hate to think of how many years it's been. You could come with me, if you want."

"No, I already told Honey I'd stay with her whenever you're gone and she said she's looking forward to it. Aren't you girl?" Dana says as she follows the large Golden Retriever across the bridge and up the basalt flow towards the path through the woods.

Suddenly, Honey stops, lifts her snout to the north and growls viciously as she stares towards the north cliffs. Startled, Dana says, "Ann? Do you see what Honey sees up there? Somethings really bothering her."

Coming beside the dog, Ann says, "What's the matter, girl? Do you see anything? I think I do but I'm not sure. Look along the cliff tops. See anything? Your eyes are better than mine."

"Yeah, there's something on top of the cliffs. Look, are there people at your cliff kitchen? Holy cow, Ann, there're four and they're waving their arms over their heads. Do you recognize any of them?"

"Not from here. No one I know would come unannounced. Besides, people need the code to the gate's lockbox or to know to call ahead. Those people must have walked down from the north or came around the locked gate and walked down the lane. I never give out the code and unlock the gate from the house around the time I'm expecting someone so it swings open for them. I locked it right after you got here last night. Who are they, Honey? Friend or foe?"

Instantly, the dog bares her teeth, barks fiercely and takes off through the trees. At the moment the dog starts running, so do the people on the cliffs as if already feeling the bite of the dog. Ann and Dana run up the basalt slope and turn up the trail in through the woods.

Running as fast as they can, Ann only slows down to scoop up the handle of the picnic basket, then she runs after Dana. Both women catch glimpses of Honey as the dog leaps over fallen logs as she zig-zags through the thick forest. Nearing the intersection where the beach trail meets the house trail, they see the dog has stopped. As they watch, Honey crouches low and stares at something in front of her.

Running as fast as they can, the sister finally come to where they can see the trail ahead of them. It is also when they can see who is standing at the trail's junction. Seeing the dog's hackles are raised from the nape of her neck to the base of her tail, Ann grabs Dana's arm and hisses, "Who the hell are they? Three men and a woman, all about the same height, the men are chubby and the woman's skinny as a rail. Hey, isn't there something familiar about that woman?"

Dana asks, "Yes, I see what you mean... what the hell."

Ann says with a shake of her head, "Two younger twins with their parents. Who is that woman...?"

Dana laughs, "Son of a bitch... Ann, it's the bitch from our past. Do you see what I mean?"

"Oh, fuck. Let's find out what they're doing here." Ann says and as she steps onto the trail, she shouts, "Stay, Honey. Stand guard and stay."

When she shouts this, three of the people shout back, "Call off your dog." "We've here to visit you." "It's good to see you."

One of the young men stands silent, glaring at the dog, as the sisters walk towards the family. When they get next to Honey, the youth lowers his head as if to run and butt them into eternity. However, he is stopped by the woman who puts out her arm and steps in front of him. 'Hey there, you two. Remember me? I'm your cousin, Lydia Parsons. Remember how much fun we had when you visited my folk's farm?"

Not answering the woman's questions, Ann and Dana stand on either side of Honey and hear the low growl coming from deep within the dog. Moving as if one, the dog and sisters walk up the trail several feet before they stop. Turning, they face the woman and Ann hisses, "Lydia Parsons? Good lord, Dana, its Lester and Hana's oldest. You remember... the bitch."

"Yessss," Dana breathes out, "What the hell brings that her here?"

"It can't be good. Get ready to roll with her punches. Remember, she throws shit with a smile on her face." Ann says as she taps Honey's head and the dog's growl comes loudly from her throat causing the family of four to back down the trail a few steps. The sisters stare silently at the four people for several more seconds.

Suddenly, Ann claps her hands and points up the path to the house and Honey rushes up to the trail, then vanishes into the steep hillside forest. When the dog can no longer be seen, Ann says, "Lydia, Lydia, of course I remember who you are and who you were. I see you've collected a family along the way. Now, tell us how did you get onto my property? The entrance gate to my driveway from the county road is fenced and gated with a lockbox alarm that needs a code to open it. How did you get past that? Lydia?"

At the sound of her name, the woman steps away from her family and says, "Dear Ann, I'm so glad to see that you remember me. Yes, I'm Lydia Parsons, Lydia Johnson now. This is my husband Jake Johnson and our two sons, Max and Mike. My mother was Hana Parsons, your mother's sister. We're here to extend our hands in friendship."

Squinting at the woman, Ann says, "Know this, Lydia, when I said I remember you, I meant I remember everything about you. Everything and none of it is good. So, Lydia, I repeat my question, how did you get onto my property? You are not welcome and you are trespassing. I insist you hike back the way you came and leave here. Do you hear me, Lydia? Get you and your family off my property. Right now. Go. Don't say another word, just go."

To the sister's surprise, Lynda starts marching up the path. As she passes where the sisters are standing, the three men follow her and glare fiercely at Ann as they pass. When the four are half way up the hill, Lydia suddenly stops and waits for everyone to catch up with her.

Not stopping, the sisters pass the woman, who shouts, "Stop. Please. Listen to me. Ann? Dana? We're family. Doesn't family mean anything to you? Please, Dana? Get your sister to listen to me? You were the nicest of all my cousins. Ann was always the most stubborn one."

Dana's eyes flash wide-open as she says, "Oh that's a good one, Lydia, but it sure won't make any goody points towards getting your way. My God, you still are the dumbest rock on the beach, aren't you?"

Ignoring the remark, Lydia says, "Listen, you two, I need to make you both listen to me. You don't know the good news we came to tell you. We're your new neighbors. Yes, we are. Jake and I bought the full section on top of this same mountain. We built our lovely retirement home at the very top. Yes. Yes, we did. Straight up this trail and about a mile more. Right at the very highest point. We're there. We got it months ago and, at that time, I saw on a map, in the realtor's office, that our land was directly above the very beach where your Daddy, James

Anderson, built his family cabin. When I saw the beach was called Redcliff's Beach, I just knew it had to be where you lived. One of my most happy memories is when my folks brought our family for a visit. It was years ago and such a beautiful sandy beach, back then. It's so different, now. What happened to change it so much?"

Staring at the woman, a wide grin comes over Ann's face and she begins to laugh. Turning towards Dana, she points up the trail and both sisters start running up the steep path and neither stops until they reach the flatness of the driveway that connects the county road to the house. Giving each other a quick hug, both sisters walks towards the house.

It's then that Honey comes running to greet them and turns to bark at the house. When they see what the dog is barking at, the two sisters are stunned. Sitting in front of their garage door is a very shiny gold colored, very large Mercedes executive sedan. As if she owned the car, Honey walks back and forth along the car's side. Then the animal stands next to it and her wagging her tail thumps against the driver's door.

Groaning, Dana says, "Well, now we know how they got in here."

Ann nods, "We certainly do, don't we, Honey?"

Grinning broadly, Dana says, "How did they ever get it through the locked gate?"

Ann doesn't answer, but goes directly to the driver's door on the large car and opens it. Inside, she sees keys were left in the ignition. Grabbing them, she backs out from the vehicle, holds them out for Dana to see, then slams the car's door and shouts, "Who the hell belongs to this awful clunker and why is it parked on my property?"

As she shouts, she slips the car keys into her jean's pocket. The next moment, the chubby twins come stomping onto the driveway one at a time. Gasping for breath, they fall dramatically to the ground and moan loudly. Their mother walks slowly off the trail and over to where the sisters stand beside the car.

Trying to speak as she come towards them, Lydia gasps between each word, "Get… away … from… car." Then, she leans across the trunk end of the wide car breathing hard.

Enjoying the sight of the family trying to recover from their hike up the steep path from the beach, Dana chuckles and says, "Well, sis, that's three of the beasts. Where the hell is the biggest whale of all?"

"I'm thinking that guy may have died on the way up, he's so out of shape." Ann answers.

Smiling, Dana says, "Dear God, let's hope not. It'll cost a bundle to have him hauled out from there."

Looking at her watch, Ann says, "We'll give the jerk another minute. By then he'll either be up here or dead down there."

In exactly one more minute, Jake Johnson staggers out from the path and down the driveway to where his wife, Lydia, leans against the car. Holding onto his wife, the man has the sense to wait until he breaths normally before speaking. At that time, he growls, "I heard what you called my car. This Mercedes is no clunker. This sedan is the top of the Mercedes line. What you call a clunker, cost over a hundred and fifty grand and I paid cash. What the hell do you drive?"

Smiling sweetly at the indignant man, Ann says, "None of your damn business, Johnson. Now, get your family into that jewel of a clunker and drive your family off my property."

"No...Wait. Wait. Don't fight with her." Lydia Johnson shouts as she pushes her husband aside causing him to stagger several steps backwards. When she is standing between her husband and the sisters, the woman chokes out, "Stop threatening her, Jake. Being a bully won't get what we want. Don't you see you can't achieve anything that way?"

Turning to the sisters, Lydia says, "Ann? Dana? Please? Give me a few minutes to explain why we're here. Can't I talk to you before we leave? It's been years since we've seen each other. Please, Dana, talk some sense into you sister. Would you please tell her to listen to me?"

"Leave Dana out of this, Lydia. You're on my property uninvited. I have told you to leave several times. We have nothing to discuss. You've known where I've lived for the past thirty years, Lydia. I received a Christmas card from you every year for ten years after I moved here. Suddenly, you buy the top of the mountain where my house sits and come down here unannounced. Why do you suddenly want me to be part of your family? Is it for the same reason you bought property at the top of the same mountain? What do you think of that, Dana?"

"I'd think she discovered their mountain of land has no beach access. Why else would she come down here after all those years? She wants you to let a road down so they can say their land has beach rights. Lydia said she saw a map at the same realtor's. My guess would be that was why they bought the top of the mountain in the first place. She thought she could con good old cousin Ann into giving her beach rights."

"Yes, that's my thinking entirely. Sure, Lydia, why not? I'll gladly let a road be bulldozed through my property. It would only mean allowing several hundred people a day come down to the beach and go onto the cliffs and ruin the kitchen area I worked so hard to build years ago."

"Oh, darn it, it's so hard for me to say no, Ann. Didn't Lydia say I am the most gullible, no, she said I was the more reasonable of the two of us. Isn't that right, Lydia? Well, here's my answer to your request. ABSOLUTELY NOT. Of course, that's only my answer. Ann must speak for herself."

"Sorry, Lydia, my answer is the same as Dana's. NO, NO, NO. NOT EVER. Did you hear me, Lydia? Was I clear enough for you to understand my decision?"

"What you should have realized by now, Lynda, is that though Ann may not have thought of you over the years, I have. I never forget the day that you and your siblings nearly killed Ann when she was a small three year old. Remember that day, Lydia? Aahh, I see by your intense blush that you do.

"When Dad drove us out to what he called 'Lenny's stump farm', Ann and I were thrilled to see all our cousins. We followed you kids everywhere as you showed us the farm animals and took us through the barn. Then, you went out front to where several new lambs were being held in by an electrical wire fence. When, Ann got too close to the electric wire fence and it gave her the same shock it had the lambs and she shrieked. Still she didn't leave as she wanted to watch the lambs. I moved her back from the wire. But you and the others began grabbing hold of the fence and counting to three and I saw that the flashing red light on a post matched your count and realized when the light went off there was no electricity in the wire. So I began to do grab that wire and count in time with you.

"Little Ann only saw that it didn't hurt me and grabbed the wire with one hand and was shocked by the electricity. When it did, you kids told her to hold the wire with both her hands. That made Ann part of the fence and she couldn't let go of the wire.

"My screaming for help brought the adults onto the front porch to see Ann hanging onto the wire, jerking up and down. Dad grabbed her and also got caught by the electricity. It was Lenny, your father, who knew to pull the wire fence plug from the electrical socket on the power box. He grabbed Ann and blew into her mouth until she began to breathe again. That's what I remember, Lydia. I remember that you, the oldest of us kids, knew to pull the plug on the electric box and didn't. You would have let Ann die. Your Dad was the hero that day."

"Oh, for heaven's sake, Dana, that was years and years ago. I was only ten, a child. We were all children," Lydia shouts. "Besides, my Dad spanked me for the longest time and sent me to bed without any dinner. If he saved Ann, did you ever thank him for that?"

Giving the woman a disgusted look, Dana says, "Yes, I did, Lydia, I thanked Lenny on the anniversary of that day every year he was alive. Your Dad and I became good friends. We wrote each other regularly and saw each other yearly, whenever I was in the area. He and Hana came to my show opening at the Portland Museum. I wouldn't be surprised if Lenny is watching us right now. He must be very sad to see you up to your same old nasty tricks."

"Okay, Dana, enough of that. On this point, I agree with Lydia. That hot wire happened a long time ago. What I want to know is in the here and now. Why Lydia? With all the beautiful land in the State of Oregon, the state where you lived most of your life, why buy land in Washington State. If beach rights are what you want, Oregon is where to buy land near the coast. In that State, the beaches are public domains as part of the highway system. Here in Washington beach rights are attached to the land adjacent to the beach and privately owned."

Dana exclaims, "Hey, that's right. Why do you want access to Redcliff's Beach? It's nothing but rocks and boulders. What's the benefit for you? Oh sure, of course, to sell the mountain top with beach rights would get top dollars per acre."

Shaking with anger, Lydia yells, "Jack and I bought that full section at the top of the hill for our own use and built our summer home up there months ago. We plan to retire there. It has a great view of the ocean. In fact, we look right over your property. All I would ask is for a path down to one of you beaches to the north."

"Lynda, please stop this. I already gave you my answer. The only thing I want now is to know is how the hell you got that beast of a car down my lane. My property is fully fenced and posted. There is a steel gate with a lockbox that controls the only entrance off the county road. You had to either cut through the fence or break open the lockbox before you could pass the gate. Oh, my God, Lydia, that's what you did, didn't you? You broke open the lockbox in order to slide the gate open."

Shocked, Dana shouts, "Holy shit, Lynda, didn't you see the signs that said the lockbox is secured by an interior alarm system? That means when the box is smashed, the blow triggers an electric alarm that goes to the security firm and they contact the nearest Sheriff's office. Just like that electric fence around the lambs, that box sent pulses back to a system and if the pulse is broken, alerts are sent to the local police."

"How stupid of you, Lydia. We've been with you about an hour and, if you broke open the lockbox much before that, someone from our County Sheriff's office in Hoquiam is on their way. If you know what's good for you, Lydia, you'll get your family into that clunker and get the hell out of here before they get here. There's a steep fine for breaking one of those boxes."

Shaking her fist at Ann, Lydia shouts, "I'm not going until I've had my say, Ann. It's time I tell my side of things. We bought the land for our own home. Once we saw how beautiful the view was, we decided to sell off a few acre sized lots. Our boys have passed their realtor exams and we contracted with a lumber company to clear most of the land.

Once it's cleared and the road marked out, the boys will start selling the lots. Beach access would be a plus and up the value of each lot. We plan to offer you a percentage of each sale. It would mean a lot of money for you both. Ann? Dana? Please reconsider my offer."

Ann smiles sweetly at her cousin and says, "Lydia darling, why didn't you say that in the first place. How could I possibly refuse that? A fifty percent cut from each sale? Of course, let's shake on that. Fifty-fifty split sounds fair to me, does it change your mind too, Dana?"

Before Dana can answer, Lydia's twin sons, shout at their mother until she screams, "Shut up. Shut up. Shut up, both of you boys. Shut up the hell up. Get into the car. I will make this deal with Ann without your damn input. Go. Now."

Then, Lydia says, "Ann and Dana, please, you both must realize that a fifty percent cut is completely unreasonable. However, I would consider a fair amount such as ten percent. Since your forest will also be cut down, you'll make millions from the timber sale. That's a given. So, reconsider my request and let's cut these trees down. After all, it would be terrible if one of our own bonfires sent sparks down over your land and it caught on fire. After all, anything can happen when these strong offshore winds come this time of the year."

"Are you threatening us, Lydia?" Dana asks.

"Of course not, Dana. It just that's how things happen. Naturally, I thought that if you take my generous offer of five percent and allow us to bulldoze a road down to your cliffs, everything should stay safe and tidy. In fact, better yet, let's join our two properties together. My brother Jess is a lawyer and has contracts ready to finalize any deal you decide to make with us. Please, Ann? Dana? You know I'll make it worth your while. I'll guarantee that personally."

Smiling, Ann nods her head slowly and says, "Lydia, Lydia, Lydia, you're still the same old malicious Lydia. First, you want a path to the beach. Then, it's a bulldozed road. Now, we should join our two properties together. Of course, we should also believe how fair and square your offer would be. No, Lydia, never would either Dana or I consider becoming partners in your land scam. Absolutely not. It'll never happen. Besides, Lydia, right this very minute, you have a bigger problem. Turn and look down my driveway. Do you see that large SUV, with flashing red and blue lights, speeding towards us? My guess is that vehicle belongs to our County Sheriff and I'll bet he's come to say more than a polite Hello to you and your family."

Dana slaps her thigh and laughs, "Well, howdy folks. Yes, indeed, that's Cliff Deaton's SUV, all right. Now, we'll find hear exactly how you got that tank of a car down to our house. Which was it, Lydia? Did you figure out the lockbox code or did you smash through the gate? Whatever you did set off the alarm."

"Oh shut the hell up about that damn alarm. We didn't hear any alarms go off. Did we, Jake?" Lydia asks her hubby standing right beside her. "Besides, what can that country hick do to us? We don't live in his jurisdiction. Jake? Say something, Jake?"

Hearing his name seems to wake the big man from his stupor and, when he sees the SUV racing towards him, he yells, "Shut up and get in the car. Now, Lydia, do it now."

Instantly, the woman runs to the other side of the big car and climbs inside the passenger side just as the large silver SUV slows to a stop at the edge of the cement parking pad a few feet from where the sisters stand. Inside the vehicle, Ann sees a man's familiar face through the tinted windshield and she smiles at him. Seeing that, the man winks and both sisters smile in response. For a few seconds, the man studies what he sees. Then he shifts the SUV into reverse and backs across the driveway to completely block the way out to the county road.

When the SUV's door opens, a muscular thickset man emerges and stands towering over the top of the vehicle. After adjusting himself to full height, it is clear to all the man's build fills out his crisply ironed shirt with its silver buttons and badges glinting in the sunlight. Stepping towards the two sisters, Sheriff Deaton nods and says, "Good afternoon, ladies. I believe I got here in time to help you settle some sort of dispute. Am I right?"

Grinning at the man, Dana points to the large car and the family inside it. Raising his eyebrows, the Sheriff ambles past the sisters to the front of the gold Mercedes sedan and squats in front of the car's bumper for a full minute. Then he stands slowly and peers over the hood through the windshield for another minute. Finally, he raises his right hand, points at the driver and with two fingers motions for the man to come out of the car.

For a full minute, Jake stares through the windshield at the man motioning for him to get out of the car. When Sheriff Deaton does not move or change his stance but continues to waggle his fingers at the windshield, Jake slowly opens the car door and moves off the car seat. Dropping low, as if to hide behind the open car door, Jake stares at the officer through the car door window.

Finally, Jake stretches himself to full height, adjusts his clothes and steps away from the car door. The next moment, the paunchy man smiles broadly and reaches out his right hand out as he loudly exclaims, "Howdy there, Sheriff? Jake Johnson here. Is there something I can help you with at this time?"

Giving a slight shake to the extended hand, Sheriff Deaton says, "Howdy, Jake. Sheriff Cliff Deaton here. I'd like you to mosey over past me and stand by my side. That's good. Now, sir, I need your opinion on what might have caused those deep gouges along your car's front bumper. Do you own this car?"

Still grinning, Jake replies, "Oh yes, this grand golden Mercedes is all mine. Bought and paid cash for. What can I do for you, Sheriff?"

When the Sheriff simply points at the front bumper on the large sedan, Johnson bends forward as if to look for what the Sheriff sees. Then he looks over at Ann and Dana who are also bending close to the bumper. It is the sisters who shout with dismay when they see the smears of grey/green paint mixed in the gold paint of the Mercedes gouged and scraped front bumper. "You stupid jerk. You crushed the gate's security lockbox. That's how you got this beast of a car down my driveway. That grey/green paint is the same as on the lockbox. What a creep you are."

Continuing to study the scrapes, Dana reaches out as if to touch one of the deeper scrapes on the bumper and Sheriff Deaton barks, "Don't touch that, Dana. That's evidence."

Then turning to Jake, he says, "How about it, sir? Can you explain how you got these marks on your car?"

"Oh, those old things. Happened days ago while driving the Columbia Gorge. Hit large boulders that fell on the freeway. Near the Dalles. Slammed into a couple big boulders. I got an appointment later this week to take care of those scrapes. Insurance, you know. Hate the cost but love it when you need it." Jake says following with a loud hollow laugh.

When Sheriff Deaton only stares at him, Johnson turns bright pink. After a few seconds of silence, the Sheriff turns to Ann and Dana and says, "Do either of you know these people? Are they friends of yours?"

Ann shakes her head and says, "No, Cliff, not friends. The woman in the car happens to be a cousin of ours from ages past. She and her family came are uninvited intruders. Dana and I first saw them from the trail coming back from the cabin. Then, they were on the cliff tops near the kitchen. When we got to them on the trail, we asked how they got in and they wouldn't tell us. When I demanded that they leave, they would not leave. When I saw your SUV coming down the lane, I could have cried I was so relieved."

As tears fill Ann's eyes. Dana sees her sister's distress and she picks up what they were told by Lydia Johnson. "It seems the family bought a full section on top of this mountain. Now they want a road down to access the beach which would double the land's value. When Ann told her no, Lydia, the woman in the car, threatened to build fires when an offshore wind was blowing and burn us out."

Looking at Lydia Parsons Johnson, the Sheriff points at her through the windshield and says, "Ma'am, please step out of the car."

When it seems Lydia isn't going to respond, the Sheriff barks at Jake, "Get your wife out here. Now."

Screaming through the open driver's door, Jake yells, "Damnit, Lydia get your ass out here. This Sheriff's not going to play your kind of games."

At that, Lydia pops out from her side of the Mercedes and smiles sweetly, then says, "How can I help you, officer?"

Smiling at the woman, Deaton asks, "Tell me Ma'am, did your family get the code to the lockbox from Ann before you came down? Yes? So, tell us the numbers. You didn't write them down? No? Okay, ma'am, I'm through playing games. If you know the numbers, say them to Ann. If you can do that, you and your family may leave right now. Do you understand me? Ma'am?"

Thrusting her chin out, Lydia steps forward and says, "Listen you, I'm Ann's cousin from Oregon. We built our home on the top of this mountain to be close to her and Dana. We're family. We came down to talk to Ann about a plan for a road down to one of her many beaches. Didn't we, Jake? Boys?"

When there is only silence from her family, Lydia turns and screams, "Tell the Sheriff that I spoke the truth. Do it now, you dumb shits."

Frowning at the woman, the Sheriff holds one hand up to stop her outburst and says, "Lady, I asked you a simple question. Did Ann give you the numbers to the lockbox? Yes or no. Can you tell me what they are? Do you understand simple English?"

Without answering, Lydia backs around the long car, then come forward and stops beside her husband. Then, the two fold their arms across their chests and stare silently at the Sheriff. Watching the pair, Deaton says, "I'll take that as a no you didn't get the code from Ann."

When the couple stays silent, Deaton turns to Ann and says, "Now, I'll ask you the same question. Ann or Dana, did either of you ever give out the code to your gates lockbox to these or other persons?"

"No. I never give it out. If friends come to visit, they know to call before or when they get to the gate. At that time, I buzz the lockbox from the house. When I asked Lydia how they got past the gate, she just changed the subject or didn't answer just as she did now. Looking at that messed front bumper it simple to guess how they got past the gate. How does the lockbox look?"

"Totally trashed." the Sheriff answers as he waves at the two patrol cars parking behind his silver SUV. As the officers get out of their cars,

Deaton continues, "Here're my guys. I'll turn these people over to them. After they've gone, I need to get a written statement from each of you sister on how this morning went down. It's been over two hours since the lockbox alarm company reported your box had been ruptured. How long would you say they've been here, Dana?"

Looking at him for a long moment before she answers, Dana says, "I'm not really sure. We were down in the cabin on the basalt point for a couple hours this morning. It was nearly noon when we started up the path along the shoreline and Honey began barking at something up north. It was when she raced away from us, that we saw four shapes moving along the clifftops. As neither of us expected anyone, we didn't know who they might be and were very cautious as we ran after Honey. When we got to the point on the path where we could see Honey, she stood in the middle of the path up to the house and was growling at four people."

Nodding, Ann says, "Yes, that's how I remember it also. That would have been over an hour ago. Since they were on the cliff tops, they could have come here earlier. Because of the lockbox, I never lock the house unless I'm off my property. The Johnsons may have even been in the house for some time before they went down to the cliffs. I guess I'll need to check and make certain nothing has been disturbed."

When Lydia hears Ann's remarks, she screams, "We're not thieves. We did go inside, but only to use the bathroom. Oh and the boys took a couple bottles of beer from the fridge. They drank those out on the deck. You'll find both bottles out there. It was a lovely day, so we waited on the deck for a while. Then the boys saw that picnic area on the top of the cliffs. That's when we took the trail down as we thought Ann might be down there. We didn't know Dana was even here. We didn't steal anything."

As she ends her rant, Lydia moves away from Jake and goes behind the vehicle. Seeing her do this, the Sheriff points at her, turns to the deputies and quickly updates them on what he knows about the situation and the scrapes and gouges on the Mercedes front bumper. Then, he says, "Each of you take one parent and one of the kids in your car. Be certain the inner video cameras are turned on. Doug Hanson is bringing the county tow-truck. He'll take photos of both the lockbox and this car and take both of them back to the holding pen. Was he there when you two got here? Good. I'll stay until he leaves and follow once I get the sister's statements.

"Place each adult in a separate room. Interview them separately once they've called their lawyer. Tell Mary to watch the young ones until someone comes to get them. The parents will be held overnight unless a judge will set bail. Be certain to record everything. Use timed and dated video."

Standing a few feet in front of the Sheriff, Lydia and Jake hear what the Sheriff says and move close together. Then, Jake thrusts his chest out and begins yelling, "Hey, you country bumpkin, you don't' have enough to hold us. You don't know a thing about anything. I want my lawyer."

"Call him. Right now. I can see your holding you phone in your left hand. So call him right now. Tell him to meet you ASAP at the County Sheriff's office in Hoquiam, Washington. Tell him you'll be there in an hour or so and to bring bail money. As for not having any evidence on anything, Mr. Johnson, the gold paint from that Mercedes yours is all over that trashed lockbox at Ann's gate. I'm sure you know that Mercedes' paints are patented and used only on their cars. The same goes for the lockbox company's green. I'd say that's evidence enough to put you two away for a few weeks to many months. Remember, tell your lawyer to find a judge to set bail and to bring the money. This looks to be an open and shut case."

Both deputies go to opposite sides of the Mercedes, open the doors, ask the young men their names and read each their rights. Then the young men are asked to step out from the car and to follow one of their parents. Now, totally subdued, family of four silently walks behind the deputies to the patrol cars. Once each parent and a child are settled inside both cars, the doors are shut and locked.

Glancing at Dana, Ann begins to giggle. "Dear God, I hope Mom is watching us right now. Seeing Lydia being arrested would make her so happy."

Dana smiles and says, "Yeah, it certainly would. Don't you just love it? That bitch of our family is finally getting her just-due."

Catching the look of surprise on the Sheriff Cliff Deaton's face, Ann says, "Sorry, Cliff, but that family was a sharp thorn in our family's side. Their mother pecked at our Mom until Mom finally told her to go to hell. I'm so amazed that Lydia thought she could simply show up and I'd go along with her plans. It's hard to explain how satisfying it is to see her taken away in a patrol car."

"When's the last time you heard from her?" Cliff asks.

"Over ten years ago. She used to send a Christmas cards which I never answered. What will happened to her and the family?"

"Smashing the lockbox and crashing through the gate is a felony, considered as breaking and entering. The consequences can be stiff. Besides those charges, the lockbox company will sue for full restitution for the old box and full payment for the installation of the new box. Then, there's you. You could have the choice of several actions. Talk to your lawyer about those. In fact, you should give your lawyer a call today. Protect yourself against any civil case those two might counter attack on you. All in all, your cousin and family could end up paying a lot of money to the court and the company. It'll be up to the court to decide what else goes with the breaking and entering. Anything from a severe scolding and community service to several months of jail time. It really depends on how good their lawyer is and who the judge is."

Smiling, Ann looks up at the tall man, "I'm telling you, Cliff, I was never so glad to see anything in my life as I was when your SUV came roaring down my drive. Thanks for responding so quickly. Dana and I were shocked to see them standing on the trail from clifftops. We had no idea who the hell they were until we got close enough."

Pausing to look down at Honey, Ann says, "My dog is the hero. She kept them from getting back up to their car."

"When the alert came in, I thought it was just a short in the wire. But when I saw that lockbox post, I decided you two could be in deep trouble. I'm glad it turned out the way it did. Now, how about we go inside and get your statements written down? I sure wouldn't turn down a cup of hot coffee."

As they walk into the house, Ann says, "Dana, take Cliff into my office and write your statement while I get the coffee going. I'll cut up the sandwiches in the picnic basket and that pie you baked last night."

# SEVEN

## *June 10<sup>th</sup>—Liz*

**LIZ** slaps the golden stone in the north cliff face and shouts, "I declare this run good and done." When nothing changes, she looks down at Kip and says, "Guess we do business at home today, kiddo. Do you want to watch these volley ball players or race me back to the house?"

*Let's stay and talk to Rudy Sloan for a while. Okay? He's sitting right over there.*

"Rudy Sloan?" Liz exclaims as she stares at the grinning Elkhound. "Why would I go talk to Rudy Sloan?"

*Maybe because he's our neighbor and now sitting right next to us and can hear you.*

As soon as she hears Kip's response, Liz turns to look at the edge of the granite slab and hears the man's smooth deep voice say, "Hello Liz. Are you trying to decide whether to speak or flee? I didn't mean to butt into your daily run, I just thought it was time to get to know you better. Why don't you do as Kip suggest and sit down beside me, Liz?"

Staring at the man, Liz feels her face get warm. However, Kip walks to the man's side and lays down on the stone next to Rudy Sloan and he says, "Come on, Liz, don't be shy. Look at Kip, He wouldn't lay next to me if he didn't think I was okay. We're old buddies. I admit that I followed you up here this morning as I couldn't think of any other way to get your attention."

Looking down at to Kip, Liz steps off the side of the granite slab and sits next to the dog and thinks,

*Traitor.*

*Oh, hush. Enjoy the sunrise. We hardly ever get to see our own dimension's glorious mornings.*

*Yes, please do that. Besides, I'm a very nice person.*

Looking at first the dog and then at the man's smiling face, Liz bursts out laughing and says, "Okay, I give up. Are you both talking to my head? If so, Mr. Sloan, it can only mean that you're more than a retired vet and writer of articles for a magazine I read in the vet's office. So before we go any further, explain yourself."

As she speaks, Liz watches Rudy run his fingers through Kip's thick fur and the two look as if they're old friends. At the thought, Liz laughs, "Well, now, I'd say you two are far better friends than I have ever imagined. Right?"

Looking up at her, Kip says,

*Of course. I told you last week that he and I play ball when you are working on your book. Rudy loves dogs and says I'm one of the great ones. Are you jealous?*

Without commenting, she squints at the man on the other side of her dog. When Rudy sees her puzzled look, he clears his throat and says, "Look, Liz. It's been three months since I've moved to Redcliff's Beach and each morning I've seen you and your fine dog run up the beach to this granite slab, slap that golden stone in the cliff face and yell something. Some of those mornings you vanish. Some of those mornings you don't. So what's the deal? Where do you go? More importantly, why do you run up here every morning?"

Surprised and a bit pleased by both his curiosity and his deep voice, Liz is a little undone by his questions. Without answering, Liz studies this man of average height, muscular build and cleanly shaven head. Though he is no more than a few feet from her, she does not speak.

Finally, Kip says,

*For heaven's sake, say something or he's going to think you are stupid.*

Frowning, Liz looks at the animal and thinks,

*Kip, why did you let this stranger get so close to you? Are you ready to leave me for him? I don't know the man. I resent that you've brought him here without discussing this with me. Remember what a mistake you made about your Dr. Dan Parker? You thought he was perfect for me. I will not let you choose the people in my life, Kip, stop it now.*

*Well, you know him already. He's our neighbor to the south and my good friend that throws my red tennis ball every day.*

Looking at Kip, she sees the dog is leaning against Sloan and both animal and man are smiling at her. Shaking her head, Liz says, "Well, Mr. Rudy Sloan. I am not accustomed to casual acquaintances asking such personal questions. So for now I will not give you any answers."

"Okay, that's fine. At least, you remember me. I was afraid you didn't. As you can see, Kip and I have become good friends. It's been days since the Jackson's picnic dinner and I've been going to stop by, but each time I start to come over, Kip comes over for me to throw his ball. These runs you two do daily to this granite slab seemed the only way to get together with the both of you. So I got here early enough to help those kids set up their volleyball net. Then I saw two get to the cliffs and came over to wait until you came back from wherever you'd go this morning. But, you stayed. Besides, I'm not the only person who notices you slap that stone and disappear. Several of the young people told me they've watched you do that for the past year."

"So, okay, it's no secret that I do the run, slap my touchstone and vanish. Just because it's become common knowledge, doesn't mean I'm going to answer your questions today. I need to trust someone before I tell the story of my life. Even though you and Kip may be friends, you're a stranger to me. Our chat at the Jackson's picnic was very brief before you allowed those two new ladies to sweep you away. I see them walk down to your place to chat you up even while you're tossing the ball for Kip. I would think they are enough female interaction for you."

"Those are too eager. I'm attracted to a more standoffish person who has a brilliant mind and a beautiful dog named Kip. Tell you why came today, I thought I'd invite Kip over for dinner tonight. Maybe he'll ask you to join us? If he does, I'll get him a knuckle bone and grill a steak and bake some spuds for us. Could you get there around six, Kip? I promise I won't ask any questions your mistress doesn't want to answer."

That said, Sloan grins at the two and waits. Almost instantly, Liz hears,

*Say yes. Say yes.*

Liz nods, "Now that sounds very doable. Kip can bring dessert and I'll toss a green salad. Kip loves knuckle bones."

Looking surprised, Rudy Sloan replies, "Oh, you thought my invitation included you. I'm so sorry, you misunderstood me. I was asking Kip to come for dinner, He'll have to ask you. However, it would probably be best if he would let you come and carry the salad for him."

When he says this, Liz laughs out loud and looks at Kip, "May I come with you on your dinner date at Rudy's this evening?"

*Of course, you may. Only if he'll toss the ball for me afterwards.*

"Of course, I will, old boy. Just make sure your gal pal dresses to kill, okay?" Sloan says to the dog and pauses as if listening to Kip. Then, Rudy turns to Liz and says, "Did you know that Kip comes to play ball most afternoons?"

"Yes, he told me a few minutes ago and I thought he was under the deck checking out the terns' nests down there. He says you two are friends so it seems you've passed the Kip test. However, since I don't chase red tennis balls into the surf, I take a bit longer to make friends."

"That being said, would you mind if I walk back with the two of you?"

"Well, we usually run. Want to join us?"

Rudy smiles, "No, my running days ended a few years ago when shrapnel took off my left knee. That was when I retired from the Marines. However, I do a fair to middling amble though."

*Let's amble with him.*

Surprised at the statements by both the man and dog, Liz slips off the granite slab and looks down at the man's legs. Seeing the metal running leg attached above Rudy's left knee, she says, "I know young guys who run on those contraptions. However, Kip says he wants to amble down the beach with you. So I guess I will, too."

"You'll see that it's a very pleasant way to go. But, if you want to run, go for it. I'll see you later, around six?"

Looking up at Liz with a full toothed grin, Kip says to her,

*Ambling will be perfect.*

At five thirty that evening, Liz closes her computer, takes a quick shower and changes into a flattering summer dress. As she comes down the stairs, she sees Kip lying on the golden stone under the adjoined dining tables with Honey and Dandelion beside him. Laughing at their mound of sprawling overlapped legs and tails, she says, "How do you three get any sleep all wrapped together like that?"

*It's not easy.*

Looking down at the three animals, Liz says, "Okay, who said that? It wasn't Kip."

Kip raises his head and noses the cat at his side and tells her,

*It was Dandy. She complains that Honey and I move too much.*

"Well, I hate to break up the buddy-bundling but Kip and I have a date with his old friend Rudy Sloan."

At the mentioning of the man's name, all three animals sit up and stare at Kip and she hears voices saying,

*You didn't tell us Rudy came here to be with you.*

*Will we get to see him here at the golden stone?*

*I'd like that. It's been too many lifetimes since I've had a good chat with the fine man.*

*Why don't you bring him over here to see us, Kip?*

*It all depends on how fast the humans become friends. I rushed this sort of thing a year ago and Liz reminded me that it didn't end well.*

Staring down at the animals, Liz holds up her hands and exclaims, "What the heck? You all know this man? All of you have known Rudy Sloan before he moved here last month? Hey, just a minute, Honey and Dandy, do Beth and Ann know you two talk this way? No? Well you'd better update them before too much time goes by, because I'll see them tomorrow morning and this good news is not going to be kept a secret. I just realized, has Kip given up any info about me to you familiars? How about to Rudy Sloan? How much have you told him, my fine furry friend?"

*Didn't I just introduce the two of you at the north cliffs just this morning?*

"Oh, is that how it was? You forget I met him at the Jackson's dinner. Besides, he said he's watched us and finally followed us to the cliffs to invite us to dinner. So, what else are you holding back from me? Are any more of your long lost friends going to pop into our lives?"

*Nope. Just these two and Rudy. He's the only one you're really supposed to get to know. Please, fall in love with him as fast as you can so we three can live happily ever after, forever. Do you think that's possible?*

"I'm not even going to give those words any consideration. You listen to me, my friend, whatever happens between Mr. Sloan and me happens at Liz speed, not Kip speed. Get it? Now, come on. It's time we get to Rudy's. I'll get the salad from the fridge. What ice cream did you plan to bring?"

*The salted caramel-pecan ice cream you bought the other day at my suggestion. Could you get it out of the freezer and put it in a paper bag for me to carry between my teeth?*

When both the salad and ice cream are collected, the two friends walk down the path through the dunes to Rudy Sloan's house. As they go, Liz wonders how and why Rudy Sloan moved in the house next to hers. Did it have anything to do with Kip being with her or because she was a Parallel Life of Elizabeth Ann?

As they come up the steps to the deck around Sloan's house, the slider door opens and the man himself steps out to greet them. "So you two are the reason a loud mishmash of thoughts hit me seconds ago. What's that you got there, Kip? Oh, boy, salted caramel-pecan, my favorite ice cream. It'll go great with the apple pie I baked this afternoon."

Laughing at the strangeness of the moment, Liz answers, "Sorry, Rudy. I guess I'll have to learn how to control my thoughts better. Did you actually hear what Kip and I were thinking? I'll have to remember to not think too much around you. Do you hear every though other people think when they're around you? I'm not certain if I can handle both you and Kip knowing my thoughts. At least, Kip keeps it to himself. I hope."

Then, suddenly, she knows before she asks and frowns down at Kip, "You do keep our discussions to yourself, don't you?"

*I only share things with Dandy and Honey. Just once in a while. They don't talk to their mistresses yet so I didn't think you'd mind. Does it really matter?*

Staring at her dog for several seconds, Liz opens her mouth to chastise the animal, then stops when she hears Rudy Sloan's chuckle. Turning to snap at the man, she can't contain her own mirth and the two humans roar with laughter as they follow Kip in through the open door and into Sloan's kitchen.

The two humans get through dinner exchanging polite chitchat about their lives before they met as Kip gnaws on the large knuckle bone Rudy gave him. After the dishes are cleared and stacked in the dishwasher, Sloan slices the pie, adds scoops of the pecan ice cream and hands one dish to Liz. Carrying it out to the deck, Liz sinks into a chaise lounge and sighs. Coming behind her, Rudy sets a small bowl of desert beside Kip and says, "Here you go, old guy. Enjoy."

Then the man brings his own dessert to the chaise next to Liz's and settles into it with a sigh. For the next several minutes, the two silently devour the savory dessert and watch the sun lower itself towards the horizon. When she reluctantly swallows her last bite, Liz looks at her empty dish for a few seconds. Then, looking sideways at Rudy, she pushes the bowl up to her face and licks it clean of any leftovers.

Seeing her do this, Rudy bursts out, "By God, Kip was right. You are my kind of girl." Then he grins at Liz and licks his own plate clean.

When she holds her right hand up to him, he laughs and slaps it for a high-five and they both beam at each other until they hear,

*You two are disgustingly two of a kind.*

In response, Rudy who says, "Look here, old chap, don't get so damn pushy. You'll have Liz fleeing back to her own house. Just lick your own plate clean and go to sleep when you tire of that bone. By the way, I plan to keep it over here in my fridge. You can gnaw on it after you chase the ball all next week. Okay?"

*Okay. I'll stay out of your lives. But hurry, tell each other what it is you need to know and get to where I want you to be. I'm going to take a nap. Call me when you're ready to go home, Liz.*

"Sounds like Kip has a good idea, Rudy. I'll start with the day Kip came to me last year."

"And I'll tell you where and when I first met Kip. Is that all right with you, old man?"

*Yes, say whatever you want her to know.*

Smiling at Liz, Rudy says, "Don't start until I get back with the wine and cheese." Then he quickly takes the dessert dishes into the kitchen and gets the wine and cheese from the fridge. When he sets it next to Liz, he sees her eyes are closed. Smiling as he watches her face, he thinks,

*Ah, sweet lass, you are a rare beauty.*

As his words fill her head, Liz's eyes flutter open and watches Rudy pour the ice wine into the elegant stemware. Smiling at him, she reaches for the glass he holds out to her and, in that moment, she sees a golden light flash through his eyes that sends a shiver through her. Touching her glass with his, the crystal rings with a clear ringing tone and Rudy says, "Here's to new possibilities."

Liz smiles and says, "That's a lovely thought, Rudy. Tell me a bit about how you first met Kip. Was Kip always his name? No, don't answer that. Just talk about your times together from the beginning."

"It's as good place to begin as any of them." Rudy says and begins telling his story of meeting Kip with flamboyant gesturing.

When he pauses, she asks, "Were you ever an actor or entertainer, Rudy?"

Wide eyed with surprise, Rudy grins and says, "Isn't everyone? Every day of every life is an audition, isn't it?"

"Don't get tricky with your answers, Mr. Sloan. Just give me a straight answer. I'll guess that you were an entertainer in more than one of your past lives. Was Kip always the same beautiful dog that I know? Or does he change with each life? Do you change?"

Suddenly, Rudy begins to shake his head and laugh so hard that tears roll down his cheeks and he says, "Holy moly, Liz, slow that mind of yours down. Kip warned me about how quick you are, but give me a break. Let me answer one question before you throw another at me. Okay? So here goes… I was whatever I was needed to be in any lifetime. Sometimes I was this person. Sometimes I was a woman named Mona. Yes, Mona. You think that's funny? Well, a couple of times I was the royal cat in the Royal Gardens of two tsars in Russia. My name was Gorby, short for Gorbachov. Yes, I was. Truly, I was."

Wiping the tears from his face, Rudy studies Liz as she sips the wine and he says, "I'm beginning to feel that this life is going to be the best I've ever had. I came this month as Kip knew about the plans Jill and James Anderson have for the Parallel Lives of both their daughters, Elizabeth Ann and Dana Marie during this Summer Solstice. He didn't want you to be overwhelmed by the events and thought you needed a strong human presence to hold you here and give you the emotional support he knew he couldn't. I'm so glad he called for me. I suffered a rough time in this life before he did. War is hell as they say and this old body is proof of that."

As a stray tear slips down her left cheek, Liz whispers, "Yes. It must be horrible. For that reason, I've never understand why men are so eager to fight to the death over the usually stupid things? It seems those sane ones or the Universe would intercede and correct the differences before all the hell breaks out?"

"Ah, Liz, I wish we could. The Highest Power within the Universe gave humans brains so they would think for themselves. That very independence put humans beyond the Universal power until their deaths. Brains were given to be for the good of all, but mankind keeps getting sidetracked. However..."

Leaning back into the chaise lounge, Rudy Sloan sighs and downs the last of his ice wine, then he reaches his left hand towards Liz. Taking hold of it seems so natural to her that when he lifts it to kiss, he says, "Is it too soon to ask you to join me upstairs?"

"I thought you'd never ask," Liz says as he pulls her off the lounge and he kisses her solidly and deeply on the mouth. Then, still holding her hand, Rudy leads her into his house and as they walk to the stairs up to the second story, they pass Kip lying on Rudy's sofa, his head resting on a large white pillow and they hear,

*Glad to see you two are finally getting to the good stuff. Enjoy yourselves.*

Kip's words stop Liz and she looks down at the dog and says, "What? What did you say, Kip? Where are we going, Rudy? No. Not yet. It's too soon. Let go of my hand, Mr. Sloan. What? Did you hypnotize me? Kip? Were you in on this?"

Dropping Liz's hand, Rudy looks as puzzled as she does and he slowly backs down the stairs. Looking shocked, he says, "Honestly, Liz, I thought I was dreaming. Please believe me, I had nothing to do with this. I know its way too soon for us to get intimate. Aah, Kip? Were you rushing our erogenous zone? Blast you, you damned dog. Don't you dare play the innocent with me, I know you too well, Mister K. Didn't I tell you to stay out of Liz and my relationship? I said we would move at our own pace and if things happen, they'll happen with no help from you."

By now both humans stand at the end of the sofa and glare at the dog and they hear,

*Oh come on, you two, relax. You can't blame me for everything. After all, I could tell you both were feeling warm and friendly towards each other. Besides, you are perfect for each other. Rudy accepts all your human foibles and you seem to accept his many lives. Just try to make it sooner than later, okay?"*

Looking at Rudy, Liz shakes her head and says, "That's my boy."

Taking the cue, Rudy says, "I think this calls for another glass of wine. Would you join me out on the deck, Liz? It's going to be a beautiful sunset."

"Thank you, Mr. Sloan that would be lovely. You wouldn't happen to have more of that good stinky cheese and crackers, would you? Maybe Kip would wake up enough to join us outside and we could take turns tossing his tennis ball for him."

*Yes. Yes. Yes… I'll get the ball. I'm ready when you two are.*

# EIGHT

## June 10th—Beth

**BETH** and Dandelion run into the cabin just as Nicole is sitting down to eat her cereal and sliced banana breakfast. As they come through the slider door, "Hey you two, did you run to the cliffs already? It's only six. The sun's just gotten up."

Smiling at her niece, Beth answers, "Yes, I woke early and couldn't get back to sleep. So when Dandy jumped onto the bed and told me she was ready for our run, we went out very quietly so you could sleep. I must say it's good to see you. Now that you're working with Lucy, we never seem to get together. Are you getting a feel for the work she wants you to do this summer?"

"Yes. It's turning out much more interesting than I'd thought it would be. Today I go back to the south cliffs and work around the end of that point. The tide's at its lowest by ten. I plan to get around to the other side as much as possible. I helped Lucy cover the end of the north cliffs yesterday and found some great specimens Lucy hadn't seen yet this summer. She's quite excited about what this beach is showing her. My job today is to look for the same sort of species around the south cliffs so she can compare them."

"Well, good luck. I'll bring your lunch down later if you'd like. I'm doing a quick run into Ocean Shores for groceries as soon as I shower and change. If there's anything you want me to pick up, put it on my list over on the kitchen counter. I should be back before noon. What do you want for your lunch? I can pick something up when I'm in town."

"Oh, yes, please, get me a double bacon burger from Dirty Dave's. It's an artery-blocker but delicious. I won't eat it more than once a month. Try one. They're yummy."

Laughing, Beth moves towards the bathroom and says, "Okay, I'll get two of the meals on the way home and have lunch with you on the beach. See you then."

After she strips off her running clothes, Beth looks at her reflection in the bathroom mirror and frowns. "Maybe I should get a salad instead. Middle age spread has started, that's for sure." Then she laughs and slaps her bare stomach and says, "What else can I expect at fifty? Fact is, I'm pretty fit for an old broad and the burger does sound delish."

While she showers, the bathroom gets steamy and she doesn't see the door being pushed open by Dandelion, who peeks into the shower and asks,

*Can I go to the store with you? I'll be good. I like to lay on the back window ledge and watch everything go past.*

Jerking the shower curtain aside, Beth looks into the steamy room and says, "Nicole? Did you say something? Is that you? Hello? Who's there? Show yourself to me right now. I don't recognize the voice. Who are you?"

*It's me, Dandelion, silly. I'm down here on the bathroom rug. Don't you see me?*

Looking down at the bath rug, Beth sees her cat looking up at her with sparkling golden eyes. Frowning, Beth demands, "Since when did you decide to talk to me?"

*Since yesterday. Kip and Honey were here and Kip told us it was time to let you and Ann know we can communicate with you. He told us how great it was to share things with Liz. So Honey and I agreed to start talking to you and Ann. Do you want me to do this? You've said many times that I must be your familiar as Kip was for Liz. You wondered why I didn't talk to you as Kip does Liz. So now I am. You were right, you know. I was sent here to be your guide and protect you through the Summer Solstices.*

Stepping onto the rug next to where Dandy sits, Beth pulls a towel off the shelf and dries herself, saying, "I guess I shouldn't be surprised, but I am. After all the times I've talked to you without getting any answers, now you decide to talk back."

*Yes. It feels very good to know that you hear me so clearly. So, I repeat, may I ride along with you to the supermarket?*

"Of course. However, you'll have to come inside with me. The truck will get too hot to leave you in it. I'll carry that old leather purse I used for years. It's a bit shabby but has lots of room to carry things. Would you like to try that?"

*I'd love it. Just don't get me too close to any yappy animals. I don't want to get thrown out of the store for hissing or spatting.*

Beth smiles at the cat, hangs the towel back on the towel rack and when she goes out to her bedroom, she hears Nicole's shout, "See you at lunch time. Thanks."

When she hears the front door slam shut, Beth says to Dandy, "Aren't we lucky that Nicole is here for the summer? She's such a darling, isn't she? So completely different then Dee was."

*That's why I was sent to live with her. When Nancy left with her husband, Nicole needed a friend to protect her from her mother. I came to give her the strength to be herself and told her to explain to Dee that she is a Lesbian. Then I sent her to you and you gave her the reassurance she needed to stay strong. I love living here with you both.*

Dressing in fresh denims and a cotton shirt, Beth stops to look at the large orange cat and says, "I'm so glad you did that for her. I'm even gladder that you came to live with me. I love you my friend."

*Love you too, darling Beth. Now can we get going?*

Laughing at the cat's bossiness, Beth pulls the large purse off the closet shelf and sets it on the bed, then says to Dandy, "Hop in and give this a try before you commit to the ride."

The large cat hops into the bag, then immediately then hops out and says,

*Could you put something soft in there? It's not comfortable the way it is now. The leather's too stiff on my bottom.*

"Sorry, I should have thought of that myself. See how nice it is to tell people your wants and needs?" Beth says to her cat as she folds a soft woolen scarf and slips it into the purse. "Try it now. Hmm... better? Good. Now, hop out and run down to the garage door. I'll go get my grocery list and wallet and we'll go."

When she gets to the door into the garage, Beth sets the purse down in front of the cat and says, "Hop in, Dandy. This purse is perfect for both of us. See? My wallet and keys fit in this side pocket and you have the big open part in the middle. Are you comfortable?"

When Dandy doesn't answer but simply kneads the thick woolen scarf on the bottom of the old purse, Beth nods, "Yup, I see it's perfect."

As she slings the thick strap over her shoulder, she looks into Dandy's eyes and says, "I'm excited that you actually asked to come with me, sweet kitty."

*Yes, me too, I wish I'd spoken to you before this. I always wanted to go with you but didn't know how to tell you without letting you know I could speak.*

In the garage, Beth opens the passenger door of the pickup truck and places the purse on the seat. Then she wraps the seatbelt through one of the purse's handles and clicks the belt into the lock. Spreading the purse open at the top, she says, "How're you doing? Does it work for you?"

*Yahoo, I'm ready to ride. Let's go to the store and fetch us some foods.*

Laughing, Beth hurries around to the driver's side, pushes the remote to open the garage door, then backs the pickup out to the driveway. Waiting for the garage door to shut before turning onto Shoreline Drive, she strokes Dandy's coat and the cat purrs loudly.

When they are going up the south hill and off Redcliff's Beach, Dandy begins to meow and Beth asks, "What's the matter, kitty?"

*Could I get out and lay on the ledge under the back window? I can't see a thing down here. Besides it's too dark in this purse.*

"Do you want me to move the purse back there?"

As an answer, the cat hops out of the large purse and leaps off the back of the seat onto the ledge under the rear window.

*Nope, no need. I got it. This ledge is a perfect place for me to see the world go by. Thanks.*

"You can ride there if you lay still. If I have to stop suddenly, you could get thrown off the ledge."

Half way to Ocean Shores, Dandy slips down to the floor of the cab and begins to check out forgotten things under each of the seats. Batting at leftover wrappers and pebbles, she flicks a paw at a hard candy and sends it zinging out under Beth's foot next to the brake pedal. At that same time, Beth turns around the sharp curve into Ocean Shores and Dandy screams, "Meowrr," as she rolls out from under the seats.

"Enough prowling, kiddo. Get back into the purse and stay there. Remember, Dandy, this is a trial run to see how you behave. That means both inside the truck and out of it."

Without protest, Dandy hops into the large open purse and begins to preen herself. Glancing over, Beth smiles at the lovely animal and slows the car to give Dandy a bit more time before they get to the store. When she parks the truck in front of the IGA, Beth lifts Dandy and the purse and she hears,

*Did I passing the test?*

"Oh, yes, my friend. You've been the perfect little passenger these last few seconds."

Inside the store, Beth places the large purse in the child seat of a grocery cart and pushes it down the first aisle. Almost immediately, a customer spots the cat and cries out, "Oh what a sweet face. Hi kitty, are you helping Mama shop?"

After that person, Dandy sits up in the purse and is soon the center of attention in every aisle Beth tries to go down. At first, she is pleased by how the people greet the cat as even the store manager comes by to say, "Hello, Beth. I see you've brought a friend. Know that she's welcome to come in the store as long as she behaves well."

"Of course, Mike, I told Dandy that when she asked to come today."

Taking her statement of fact as if a good joke, Mike bursts out laughing and says, 'That's a good one, Beth. I glad you talk things over with her. Wish my cat would listen like yours seems to do."

Smiling at the man, Beth says, "So far she's loving the attention, but it's certainly slowed down my progress. It's taken me twice as long to get just a few, so if you'll excuse me, I'd like to get home before noon."

Looking down at Dandy, she thinks,

*I sure never thought you'd be so charming to strangers. Try not to purr so loudly. It catches everyone's attention.*

However, a couple is looking down each aisle and when they see Dandy, they shout, "Here she is" and they block Beth's cart as they pet the cat without saying a word to Beth. Fully enjoying the attention, the animal purrs louder and coyly arches her back to receive the attention.

Finally, Beth pushes on the cart past the couple and says, "Sorry, but if I stop to let everyone pet my cat, I'll never get back home. Please, let me pass. I'm not stopping again."

When she finally reaches the rear of the store where the fish and meat counters are, the butcher greets her, "Hey, Beth, I see you've brought us a new customer. Hey, kitty. What's his name?"

"Her name is Dandelion but she goes by Dandy."

"How about a nice fresh piece of fish for Dandy? I just happen to have a bit left from fileting a giant cod a minute ago."

"Really, I'd rather you didn't give it to her. She'll expect this sort of attention all of the time. Just tell her how welcome she is and that she's the perfect cat. Aren't you, darling girl?"

*Don't push it, sweetie. Remember I have claws. I love fresh fish.*

"Oh, heck, give her this bit of fish. I won't make it a habit whenever she comes with you. Just hate it to go to waste."

Taking the small piece of fish, Beth holds it out to Dandy and the cat devours it in one bite. Smiling at butcher, Beth asks, "Dandy says thanks. Do you have the filet from that came from? Great. I'll take that and the large salmon filet here in the display case."

While Beth is waiting for her order, other customers surround her cart and oooh and aaah as they watch the cat lick her paw to clean her face. When finished with that, the cat blinks her golden eyes at those around the cart and the people tell Beth how lucky she is to have such a perfect pet.

Thanking them as she places the packages of wrapped fish into the cart, she says, "All right, folks, please let us past. We've got to get a few more things. Say goodbye, Dandy."

After that, Beth pushes the cart up and down each aisle as quickly as possible collecting the goods on her list. Finally, she heads the loaded cart, with Dandy and purse, into a checkout line. As she waits, a foursome of chattering teenage girls walks into the store. The obvious leader of the group spies Dandy sitting in the purse and screams with delight. As she rushes to the cat in Beth's grocery cart, the other girls follow and surround the cart trying to pet Dandy.

However, leader of these teens is not content to touch, she screams "Isn't this the most perfect kitty? Hi kitty. Let me hug you."

As she reaches into the purse to grab Dandy, the cat raises up on all four legs, arches her back and hisses loudly. Even so, the girl lifts the large cat into her arms, misjudging the cat's weight, and drops Dandy back onto the purse with a thud. When this happened, one swift paw snaps out its claws and snags the girl's hand as she pulls away screaming with pain. Innocently, Dandy steps back into the opening of the large purse, snuggles down and purrs loudly.

To the bystanders and Beth, it looks as if a gentle cat was attacked by a boisterous teenage girl and got told off. Only one of the girl's friends sees the four bloody lines forming along the top of the girl's hand and shouts, "You're bleeding. Yuck. Don't come near me."

The other two friends admonish both the screamer and their leader with, "Serves you right." "Never grab a strange cat." "You hurt the kitty."

The girl shouts back, "I'm really wounded. Bad kitty."

Luckily the line opens up and Beth unloads her groceries onto the conveyor belt of the checkout stand. At the same time, the four girls, forgetting what they came in the store for, stomp out through the automatic doors. From the checkout line closest to the door, a customer shouts, "Good riddance to bad rubbish." Other customers snicker or thank the man for saying what they claim to be thinking.

Waiting for the receipt from the register, Beth puts her wallet back into the purses side pocket and sees Dandy curled up inside the large open purse, sound asleep and thinks,

*That's a good cat... play the innocent. I saw that poor girl's hand. We can only hope she doesn't know where we live or you may have to stay in the house for the next week."*

*Nope, she'll doesn't and she'll forget me as soon as some handsome boy sees her hand and tells her how sorry he is for her. Too bad she was the prettiest one.*

*Well, I've always gotten along with kids coming to the beach, before this. I'm glad that both Lucy and Nicole are here this summer to keep an eye or two on things. We'll have tell them what happened and to watch for any trouble. We'll do the same.*

*Whatever you say is fine. I'm napping until we get home.*

As she sets the last grocery sacks behind the seats, Beth begins to shut the door and hears,

*Hey, I'm still out here in the cart. Don't forget to put me inside on the seat.*

Beth laughs, "Don't worry, Dandy, I wouldn't have forgotten my purse as my keys are in the side pocket. Now take your nap. I'm stopping at Dirty Dave's to get Nicole and my burgers on the way out of town."

*Okay. Thanks for reminding me of that. I need my nap. All that attention was exhausting.*

Saying that, the cat tucks down into the bottom of the large purse, wraps her long tail around her body and is asleep before Beth drives off the store's parking lot. At the junction to the state highway, she turns across the road into Dave's Drive Inn. Turning into the drive-up window lane, she orders two bacon burger meals, pays for them and waits at the last window. Looking into the rearview mirror, she sees a bright red Jeep drive up behind her truck. Seated behind the Jeep's steering-wheel is the girl who got clawed by Dandy.

Just as the girl looks ahead, Beth reaches out the window to take the sack of burgers and drinks from the server handing them out to her. Thanking the girl at the window, she slowly moves the truck out of the lane and eases up to the edge of the state highway. As she lets traffic go past, she sees the Jeep does not stop to get their order. Instead, the vehicle moves directly behind her truck. In that moment, Beth sees a short break in the traffic and gets in the space in front of oncoming cars. Racing back into Ocean Shores, she can see the red Jeep behind several cars following her.

Returning to the IGA parking lot, she finds an open slot near the automatic doors. Pulling Dandy's purse across the truck seats, she lifts the thick strap over her head. When the purse thuds against her hip, Dandy sits up and says,

*What's going on? Why are we back here? Nicole's lunch will get cold.*

As she slams the truck door, the red Jeep pulls up behind and the young woman says to her, "Lady? I'm so sorry if I hurt your cat. I didn't mean to do it. I love cats. Will you accept my apology?"

Stunned by this turn of events, Beth tells the girl, "What? Oh my dear, I don't think you hurt Dandy. I though he had scratched you. In fact, if Dandy could talk, I'm certain she'd apologize to you. Wouldn't you, Dandy? Can you say you're sorry to have scratched this pretty young woman?"

Sitting up to full height, the beautiful large cat looks at the girl and meows softly as she stretches out to be petted. "I think Dandy would like you to hold her for a moment. Would you like to do that?"

Smiling, the young woman says, "Oh, yes, please. Can you place her on my lap in here?"

Something about the way the girl phrased her request makes Beth uneasy and she says, "No, dear. I wouldn't want her to get frightened and scratch you again. Can you step out of the Jeep?'

As soon as Beth says this, she hears,

*Quick thinking. That girl is up to no good. See the looks of fear on her friends' faces. Let's go inside. If she comes, I will let her hold me.*

When the girl doesn't answer, Beth says, "Well, it's been nice talking to you. Get some those scratches cleaned. I forgot to get my meat order. We'll see you some other time. Enjoy your summer."

As she walks into the store, the store's manager greets her, "Welcome back. Did you forget something?"

"Yes, I ordered some fresh fish back at the meat counter and forgot to take it. It's good I did, as it seems that red Jeep is following me. The driver is the girl who tried to pick up Dandy earlier. The teen is parked right next to my pickup out front and wanted to hold Dandy again. I don't have a good feeling about that young woman. Is there any way you can distract them or hold them here until I drive away?"

"Why don't I go out and talk to the girl? I'm a close friend of her family and I'll put a stop to whatever she's up to."

"Thank you. I'll go get the fish I forgot to pick up. I'll see you at the checkout counter.'

As she walks to the back of the store, she smiles at the cat and says, "Dandy, I think we have a hero in our midst. Are you working your magic for us?"

*Not this time. You are the one working your magic, charming lady.*

Going back to the fish counter, Beth smiles at the butcher and says, "I was so taken aback by all the attention the customers paid to my cat that I forgot to get the salmon fillet I had you wrap for me. Did that Dungeness crab just come in? How about cleaning two of the largest ones for me?"

As she waits for her order, Beth feels a tap on her shoulder and sees the store's manager standing with the young driver of the red Jeep. The girl holds out her unwounded hand and says, "Ma'am, I want to apologize for following you. I didn't mean to scare you. I just wanted to hold your cat and tell her I'm sorry. May I hold her now?"

*Tell her yes. I'll be at my best.*

Beth smiles at the girl and says, "Thank you for your apology. I'm really sorry Dandy scratched you. I don't think she meant to do that. Remember, she's a hefty kitty so hold out both arms and I'll set Dandy in them. She weighs close to twenty pounds, so brace yourself."

As Dandy settles into the teen's arms, she purrs loudly and looks up at the girl with her slanted gold eyes gleaming. "Oh look, Mr. Stanwood, she likes me. Hi Dandy, you're a wonderful kitty. Thank you for letting me hold you." After a short minute, the girl turns to Beth and says, "Could you take her back now? She's really heavy."

Beth laughs and says, "She is that. Thank you for your apology. We hope to see you in the store some other time. Right, Dandy?"

*Right. Now, don't forget our fish.*

# NINE

*June 10th—Ann*

ANN follows the fence at the top of her property as she carefully pulls the cut limbs into piles along the ten foot swath she and Dana have cleared away from the property line. Dana follows directly behind her and piles more limbs onto those Ann places every twenty feet or so. The two woman and worked steadily every day since Lynda Johnson made her overt threat of starting a wild fire to create an opening along the fence adjacent to the Johnson's property. They reached the northern most corner an hour ago and are returning along the fence.

Stopping at the cutoff to the trail down to her home, Ann waits for Dana to catchup to her. Leaning against a fence post, she pulls her water bottle out from her day pack. Swallowing the rest of the water in the bottle, she watches Honey chase a squirrel up an old maple down the slope.

At that moment, Dana reaches for her own water bottle, unclips it off her belt and sits beside Ann. Looking down the fence line, she asks, "Are we going to clear along the fence to the south today? We've got the worst cleared to the north corner. The fence to the south is pretty open. It should be fairly safe to leave until tomorrow. The Johnson's are going to court the end of the week and I doubt they'll try anything before they're done with that. Who knows, maybe they'll get sent to jail."

"To hell with them, I'm pooped. Let's call it a day. I'll take the rest of the summer and bundle the brush and take it down to the fireplace on the cliffs. We'll have enough to last the whole winter."

Dana sighs. "I second that motion. That the five mile stretch we did to the north in three days is all I'm up to doing for a while. Let's leave the three miles to the county road for next week. I'm done."

"The brush piles have to dry a bit after last night's rain. You have to admit that swath we made looks a lot better than when we started. It's not really wide enough for a firebreak but maybe it'll do some good if that crazy bitch actually goes through with her threat. I can't thank you enough for helping, Dana, I couldn't have gotten so much done without you."

"Yes, you could have, but it wouldn't have been as much fun. Besides, it helps me feel the ownership you so generously given me and makes me realize owning property is a lot of work. I'll certainly keep in better shape than I did before. Now I know why you're always so wonderfully fit."

Laughing, Beth says, "Having the same parents helped us both that way, Dana. Have you decided when or if you're moving into those rooms in the house? I'd love it if it were sooner than later. Have you had any bites on selling your art gallery? I would think June would be the best month for getting a buyer."

"There's been a couple people talking with the realtor about the place since I put it up for sale two weeks ago. It'll take time and I don't want to leave it empty. I have a lot of traffic into the gallery and it shows the store is a good location. It'll happen soon enough."

"Let me run an idea past you. Besides having the lounge and the attached bed and bath, the lounge has a wet bar with a fridge. If you add a range you'd have a full kitchen. The back door goes into the garage and another door could easily be added out to the north deck and you'd have a studio and your own entrance for guests. The bedroom and attached bath don't need a thing done until after you move here. The garage is large enough for both our cars and a separate studio bigger than the one you have now."

"I realize that, dear. Still, I want to sell my place in town first."

"Not really, Dana. You could keep your Gallery in town to sell your work and rent out the lovely apartment you've made upstairs. Summer visitors would love the central location and you could make good money each summer."

"I like that idea, Ann. Why didn't I think of that?"

"Well, think about it now. Honey and I love having you here, so why not make it permanent, sooner than later."

Smiling at her sister and at the large golden dog watching them, she says, "Is that so, Honey? Could you put up with my being here all of the time?"

*I sure could, Dana. Ann and I love you and want you to live here with us. That way you can travel off to other places wherever you wish, but always come back to us here.*

"Did you say something to me?" Ann asks as she stares at her sister.

"That didn't come from me, Ann, it came from Honey. Look how she's staring at us. It was you, wasn't it, Honey?"

*Yes, you dummies, it was me. Yesterday Kip said Dandy and I should talk to our dear hearts. He said he enjoys talking with Liz. Anyway, Dandy and I agreed to let you in on our well-kept secret. Now I can give you both some much needed advice.*

The two sisters grab the large golden dog and pull her into their arms and hug her tightly between them. Wiggling with delight, the large dog enjoys every bit of their attention and cuddles into their arms as she licks and nibbles both of the women's faces. Laughing with glee, the sisters roll away on the ground causing Honey to bounce over them, woofing with joy.

After they stop their playful wrestling, the three lie together enjoying the peaceful quiet of the forest around them. As Ann looks into the clear blue sky, she notices a thin line of smoke wafting overhead and sits up. Pointing at the odd cloud, she looks down the property line and shouts, "Fire. Down there along the property line. Dana? Do you see the smoke? Honey? Am I seeing things?"

As she speaks, Honey point down the fence line and both sisters hear her say,

*Somebody's down there. Call the Sheriff.*

Then the dog races silently along the fence and the sister run after her. When they lose sight of the dog, Ann stops and shouts, I'm calling 911. Keep running Dana, I'll catch up with you. Hurry."

In the near distance, both Dana and Ann hear Honey barking at something at the top of the next slope. Energized, Dana rushes onward until she sees the dog pointing her nose through the fence. From there, she can see bushes moving not far from the fence line. As the brush pile moves out towards a part of the forest adjoining a meadow, Dana says, "What the hell is that thing?

Honey says,

*Those boys from over there are trying to light that pile of brush. They have gasoline.*

At that time, Ann stops beside Dana and says, "The fire department is coming. I also called the Sheriff. This isn't good, is it? I don't see anyone. I'm going to move further down the fence."

"Okay, but don't make a sound. Honey? Can you see what they're doing?"

When the two women move to pass the dog, Honey stays where she stopped and stares at the odd brush pile moving towards the fence. Blocking the path, Ann asks, "Honey? Do you see what it is over there? If not, let Dana and me past. We'll go find out what's going."

As if an answer, the dog moves swiftly to an opening cut out of the wires of the fence and barks furiously at a moving pile of branches. Ann and Dana stand transfixed as Honey pulls at the pile of brush until it seems to explode with arms and hands. Instantly, the two Johnson boys burst from the pile of branches and run back into their piece of the forest. Each is carrying a large red container which has liquid splashing out from it.

Howling furiously, Honey chases the two as they disappear into the woods. Screaming for the dog to come back, Ann and Dana clap their hands and shout. Finally, they see the golden dog race out from the dense forest and bound back through the opening in the fence.

Wild with relief, the sisters hug the dog. Then pull away and shriek, "Honey, you're coated with gasoline." "My God, we've got to wash you off."

"Honey, where did those guys go?"

*Directly to the Johnsons' house.*

"Good dog. Now go down to the house and let Ann hose you off. Don't lick anything on yourself until she does that. Do you understand?" Dana scolds the dog and says, "Give me your phone, Ann. I'll call the Sheriff again and tell him about the gasoline. Be sure to bath Honey with dish soap. That should cut the petroleum and then rinse her a long time."

Thrusting the phone into Dana's outstretched hand, Ann yells, "Honey come with me."

In the silence that follows, Dana quickly dials 911 and tells the dispatcher what they have seen and smelled. After a minute, there is a change in her voice as she says, "Hi Cliff, Thanks for taking my call. I'm still at the top of the hill. We haven't seen any more smoke after that first bit. Honey followed them back to the Johnsons' and came back smelling of gasoline. Ann's taken her down to the house to wash it off. There was a large pile of brush being piled close to this fence and Honey went crazy. That's when what looked like the two Johnson boys burst from the brush pile.

"No more smoke, but a strong smell of gasoline. We saw the two guys run holding red cans. Ann asked if there are any retardants that will neutralize gasoline. Do you know who can bring it here? Oh, good. Okay, good. Ann will meet you down at the house and lead you up here. See you then."

When she finishes talking into the phone, she calls Ann and says, "The Sheriff is calling up the county helicopter. It'll bring him to the cliffs. You need to stay there to meet him at the house and bring him up here. But he gets here, I'll go make certain whatever was making that smoke is out."

Going through the same cut out space in the fence which Honey went through, Dana goes to the pile of branches and debris left by fleeing men. Checking through the limbs for any embers she smells only a faint odor of gasoline and says, "Thank God for Honey. She must have scared those boys before they could get the liquid on the brush pile and get it lit. Those guys were going to burn Ann place down. Damn it, I was sure nothing would happened until their parents' trial was over."

When Dana's phone rings, she sees it is Ann calling. When she answers it, Ann shouts, "The fire department in Hoquiam has enough retardant to cover the area and kill the active ingredient in gasoline. Two guys will come out with Cliff in the helicopter. I've washed Honey and she will lead him up to you. I'll wait for the firemen to get their gear on and bring them up to you. It's going to cost me big time, but it'll be worth every penny. They'll pull the brush back to the meadow when through with the retardant. Keep Honey with you. Don't let her follow Cliff."

Dana snaps, "Thank God, Cliff came here last week when the Johnsons were here. When I told him what we'd found, he didn't hesitate a second and said it had to be those guys from last week."

"Of course, he didn't hesitate, Dana, don't you realize that he's deeply in love with you and wants to keep you safe? Talk to you later. Stay where I left you and Honey will find you."

A half hour later, Dana hears a throbbing sound and sees a helicopter cross the over the tree tops, heading towards the cliffs tops. Fifteen minutes after that, Honey runs off the trail coming up the slope and Sheriff Cliff Deaton is close behind. Seeing the man, she shouts, "Hey there, Cliff. I'm over here. The two guys started to come across the meadow towards the brush pile. They must have thought we were gone as they were cussing and yelling at each other. I hid behind this tree and barked, and growled and howled. I must have scared the hell out of them as they ran back across that meadow as fast as they could go.

"I barked instead of shouted as I was afraid they could tell I was only one person. When they ran, I started shouting but they were long gone. I changed my voice from high to low and hoped they think I was several people. They ran twice as fast as they did when Ann and I first saw them."

While Dana is talking, the Sheriff goes through the opening in the fence and checks the piled brush near that side of the fence. Then he tells Dana, "Stay where you are so when the firemen get up with the retardant they won't waste any time wondering what to do. Then, you and Ann take Honey back down to the house. Stay there. Wait for my call. I'll come back this way no matter what I find or do up here. Keep your phone handy. Hold Honey's collar. I don't want her to follow me. I'm going to track those guys back to where they came from. This pile of brush definitely has gas on it. I've called for backup to meet me over at their house. Don't worry. I'll see you later. Understand?"

Dana nods and says, "I'll wait for the firemen. Be careful, Cliff. Stay safe."

In answer, the man silently raises one hand, then disappears into the forest beyond. A half hour later, she hears Ann shout, "Dana? Are you and Cliff up here?"

"Honey and I'm here, Ann."

The next moment, her sister appears at the top of the trail with two men dressed in white protective clothing directly behind her. Without a word, one of the men goes through the opening in the barbwire fence and cuts off each strand, then he wraps it around the attached fence post. Then both men go through the opening and begin spraying a clear chemical over the brush pile. The man who cut the fence wire yells at the sisters, "Get yourselves and the dog out of here. This spray is caustic. Go now."

Without questioning, both sisters run down the path through the trees with Honey running ahead of them. When they reach the house, Dana runs to the front door and lets Honey in first. As she plops down on the bench beside the dining table, she gasps for breath and waves at Ann to come sit beside her.

Dropping beside her sister, Ann pants words, "I'm, going, to walk, the, property line, at least, once, a week… from now on. Maybe even, daily. At least, until we know the Johnsons are safely shut away."

"Great idea, Ann." Dana gasps, "I'll go, with, you. Not only, good exercise, but it will, help me, appreciate, the beautiful place you've given me. Can't thank, you, enough, Sis."

Smiling at Dana, Ann says, "Do you mean what it sounds like? You're going to move up here with me? Yes? How wonderful. Oh, Dana, I'm so thrilled. How about right after the Summer Solstice."

Hugging her sister, Dana say, "Oh, Ann, how can I ever repay you. My life as an artist gave me great pleasure but not much wealth. I tried to save my pennies too late in life for them to add up to much. It's such a relief to know I have a wonderful home now that I'm over the hill and sliding fast towards old age."

Seeing tears slip down Dana's cheeks, Ann wraps her arms around her sister and says, "Hey, darling, you're one of the most talented persons in the world. Look at what you've achieved. Your work is in major collections around the world, won numerous major prizes, had hundreds of gallery shows and are featured in major museums. Doesn't that tell you something about how the art world views your work?"

"Yeah, okay, I guess it does. However, that stuff doesn't pay the bills. When we saw the smoke it scared me so much, it was as if my life were going to go up in flames and I knew I had nothing to help you rebuild if your wonderful home were burned out. When you told me the county will expect pay back for the retardant, the helicopter and the two men's time, I was sick. Then I remembered a slush fund I started years ago. It's more than enough to pay the county's charges and definitely makes me half owner and motivate me to move up here, very soon. Okay?"

"That would be great, Dana. We can discuss it more tomorrow when we know what to expect. Right now, let's get in the kitchen and prepare lunch for those guys. You said they were spraying the brush pile when you left. That shouldn't take more than an hour. I wonder how Cliff is doing with those boys at the Johnsons'."

Dana nods, "Cliff said he'd call us as soon as sees those guys." No sooner than she says this, than her phone rings and she answers it, "Hello? Cliff? Are you okay? Yes, she's here with me, Honey too. The firemen are up spraying the retardant over the brush pile. Really? Holy cow, what will you do with them? Oh. I see… yes, of course, we will. You keep safe. Ann and I are fixing lunch for you and the guys when you get back. Be sure to come back here after you get things cleared up over there. Okay. See you later."

Turning to Ann, Dana says, "Cliff followed the boys' to their house and took them into custody. Seems they got covered with the fuel used on the brush pile when they ran with the open cans. The solvent slopped all over them and they were pretty sick by the time he got to them. He called in for Medivac to helicopter them to Harbor View's Hazardous Material Unit. They'd only splashed a small amount on the brush pile when they heard Honey. The second time they came, is when they ran with the cans open. That's good news as it means the retardant the firemen are spraying can be used along the fence line until it's gone."

"Am I to understand by what you said, that Cliff's coming here later? "Ann asks. "I'm so glad he's safe. There's no telling what those boys might have done to keep from being caught."

Dana nods and says, "Yes, I was so worried. God only knows if those kids will try anything more. Maybe getting Cliff's lecture about going to jail for a long time will get through to them. Honestly, Ann, I would never have dreamed that Lydia would have kids like those. She was always such a prissy bit of nothing. What do you think happened to her since we saw her all those years ago?"

"Oh come on, Dan, you saw evil in her when she didn't unplug that wire to the electric fence. You saw how her sisters and brothers grinned when she got spanked by her Dad. Those kids were thrilled and happier then we'd ever seen them. Yes. Evil was in her then and she married the same kind. How could their kids not follow suit. Dad always said that evil begets evil and he wasn't talking about Lydia, but her mother, Hana. Dad and Mom always felt sorry for Lenny and blamed her for his being an alcoholic."

Suddenly, Honey stands up in front of the sisters and says,

*Go make those sandwiches and fill my dish with kibble. Three guys are coming down the trail.*

# TEN

## June 15th—Together

**LIZ** slaps the golden stone in the north cliff face and, in that second, both Beth and Ann are next to her and shout their mantra at the same time she does. 'I declare this run good and done'. In the next instant, the three women wrap each other into a group hug and Liz shouts, "Holy cow. What's going on today? Were you thinking of me? Did Honey and Dandy come, too? Yes, they're with Kip. Kip? Why didn't you tell me we'd all be together today?"

*We familiars decided it was time to make you three understand who actually runs things in your dimensions.*

"What did he say? Liz? Was that Kip? Did he say that he wants us to know who's in charge of our dimensions?" Ann asks, "Have the animals taken charge of us? Honey? What does Kip mean? Are you in control of what I do? Honey?"

*More at times and less other times. Don't get so concerned. I only take full control the morning of the Solstice and you will not remember any of it after I do. Now enjoy this moment with your others.*

Honey's words fill the mind of Beth and she shouts, "Just a minute, does that go for you, too, Dandy? Aren't I in control of my own life?

Damn it, I know I am and that's that. The only thing I don't remember was during last year's Solstice in the crystal room. When the three of us turned in circles in the center of the fire-opal floor until we fell into a trance. When I woke up, I saw my parents go down a black hole in front of the crystal thrones. After it closed up, we simply stared at each other and were back in our homes. Now that I think of that, it seems odd that we left the cave and never talked about what happened or what we saw."

"Don't worry about Dandy controlling you, Beth. I think she's feeling a bit superior since she started speaking and you're too much in awe of it. I've known Kip was superior to me from the first day he came to me. How could I not? I saw the way the touchstone changed him from a sickly stray to this beautiful animal. It was amazing and I often ask for his opinion on a person or event confronting me. Honey and Dandy will do the same for both of you. Listen to their input on your decisions. If you respect their advice, they'll make you glad you did."

*Thank you for understanding, dear Liz. We came to assist each of you to experience what is needed for you to become the person you're to be. This summer's Solstice is to be the most important event each of you will experience. It will change your lives forever.*

Frowning, Liz says, "That wasn't Kip. Who spoke that time?"

Looking up at Kip, she sees his golden eyes glint with laughter and he says,

*That was Honey and she said it very well, didn't she? Trust is not a complex thought. We are here to lead you through the happenings in the crystal room this Summer Solstice. We are to assist Jill and James Anderson when they introduce themselves to each of you. At that time, they will gather those who are to return with them. You must trust that we, your animal familiars, love you and only have your best interests in our hearts. We will try to keep you safe from harm at all times.*

Hearing what their animal familiars have to say to each of them, the three women are so wrapped up in listening to their thoughts that they do not notice they are in a different Redcliff's Beach, in another dimension. Only when the young man sitting on the far corner of the edge of the granite slab, finally exclaims, "Hey there, ladies, how are you all? Liz? Aren't you going to come over here and talk with me? I'm so surprised to see the other two came with you. My Mom said she would try to send you back here to be with me today as it's my birthday and she wants me to apologize to each of you for shooting at you. It's really grand to see that you three came here at the same time and brought your animals. I guess I should ask you which one is which. I recognize Liz by her short hair. Which of the other two is Beth or Ann? Can you point out which one is which? Even Reilly seems confused, aren't you fella?"

At the sound of his voice, the six entities turn and stare at the young man and his large Irish setter sitting on the corner of the slab of rock. Ann shouts, "Holy cow, it's Neil Gardner. Look ladies, we're in Neil's dimension again. Hey Neil, I'm so glad to see you aren't pointing your rifle at me this time. I'm Ann Anderson, the second person you shot when I was slapping at the touchstone. I'm also the one your mother's essence spoke to when she came to my dimension. Bette told me how she and your Dad died. I was determined to never come back to your dimension, Liz said she'd try to reach you. When she did, we were all glad to think you would finally meet with your mother at the golden stone."

As he listens to Ann, the young man walks over to where she stands by the touchstone in the cliff face and holds out his hand to her. When she takes hold of it, he kisses it and says. "Dear Ann, I'm so sorry I shot at you. I thank God every day that I didn't kill either you or Beth. I'm so ashamed of what I did. Please forgive me, will you? Beth, I mean every word of this apology for you, also. Please forgive my clumsiness. I want to thank all of you for hearing my Mom's words. I especially want to thank you, Liz, for coming here that day and telling me all that Mom wanted me to know."

"Do you sit at the adjoined tables and talk with your mother every day?" Liz asks.

"Yes, every morning. Mom comes to me at that time and we talk about is to happen and I tell her about the plans I have for my life. It's wonderful to see her so often. She told me about meeting with you, Ann. She said there are several essences of other Elizabeth Anns where she is now. I know she will be going away on the Summer Solstice and I'm sure she will be happy to hear that you three came here today. Mom said I should tell you that something very big is going to happen to each of you during the Summer Solstice. Do you know yet what that is?"

"Not a thing, Neil. Our animal familiars just told us that same thing just minutes ago. It sounds as if it's going to be something big. My Dandelion only recently started to speak to my mind. Honey, Ann's dog also is doing the same. Liz is lucky, as Kip has always talked to Liz. Does Reilly ever talk to you?" Beth asks.

"Oh, yes, he's spoken to me from the first day I got him as a pup. I just thought all dogs did that with their masters. It was a shock to find out that other pets don't always do it, though there are some that do."

Stepping over to the youth, Beth tells him, "Neil. I'm Beth Anderson. I'm the first one you shot. Luckily for both of us, you were a lousy shot. The bullet hit my left arm and went clean through the flesh. My friend, Lucy Wong, cleaned and bandaged it for me. It's mostly healed now. You scared the hell out of me, young man. Like Ann, I was determined never to come here again. But, I'm glad I cane today and heard your apology. I accept it gladly and am glad you didn't mean to hurt me."

"Me, too, Beth. Mom told me how lucky I was that I didn't kill either of you as my karma would have made me relive my life over and over again. I'm so glad you came here with Liz and you accept my apology, Beth. I'm truly sorry I hurt you so badly."

Turning to Liz, Neil holds out his hand to her and says, "Liz, it's good to see you again. I recognized you by your voice when you spoke and, of course, that short hair of yours. You spent a long time with me that day trying to get me to understand about Mom. She thanks you for relaying her message to me. As I said, we meet and talk every day. She told me about her and Dad's deaths. They had just gotten back from an evening run up to the cliff face to slap the touchstone and shout our family's mantra, when the planes came at them, seeming out of nowhere. They thought they were the Navy's flight team practicing their routines. Nobody ran. People just stood where they were and waved as the planes came at them. When the guns started shooting, nobody had time to run. I found my parent's bodies on out front deck where they dropped. When I finally sat with Mom at the golden stone under our dining table, she said she and Dad were killed instantly and never suffered."

Putting an arm around the youth's shoulders, Liz says, "I'm so relieved you have talked with Bette, Neil. You mother was so distressed when you kept running away from her. When you see her again, tell her that the three of us are usually at the adjoined tables right after our early morning runs to the north cliffs. It makes me so happy to hear your family ran to the touchstone in the cliff face and shouted the same mantra my family did. It makes me think that you might be able to come through at the adjoined tables to join us at our tables. Reilly would like to be with the other animals. We're usually there around seven to nine each morning."

"I'll give it a try. It's been close to ten that I meet Mom. Reilly kept saying it was too late, but when she came through to me, he stopped scolding me. He did tell me he saw your animals often whenever he sleeps on the golden stone. I love that he talks to me, no matter how bossy he gets. I don't know what I'd have done without him here these past two years."

Beth moves closer to the youth and says. "What really irritates me about Dandy talking to me, is how often I wished she'd talk to me as Kip did to Liz. Now, when I hear her, it seems as if she's bossing me to do this or that all of the time. If I complain about her chattiness, she reminds me how often I wished for her to talk to me. Time will only tell how much I'll listen to her in the future. My niece, Nicole, was Dandy's first owner and she loves that the cat now tells her things about her life. So far she finds Dandy talking very pleasing. I so admit it depends on what events my gregarious cat is telling me about. Isn't that right, Dandy?"

As soon as she asks her cat the question, Beth and her Dandelion cat vanish from the granite slab in Neil Gardner's dimension. "Holy cow, did you see that?" the young man exclaims, 'One second she was here talking to us and the next second, poof, she's gone. Whew. That was so sudden. Did it surprise you two as much as it did me? What made them vanish at that moment? Do you think maybe Dandy did it because Beth was talking about her so much and the cat decided to show Beth who's boss? Do either of you know when you're going to vanish? Liz? Ann? Can you control it or does it just happen? Are you ever surprised by where you go?"

"Whoa, kiddo, hold up a moment, one question at a time," Ann laughs, "I'll answer just for me and say no, I don't know before I change dimensions. Yes, I'm always surprised and sometimes I'm shocked. The only places I've gotten used to shifting dimensions are at the adjoined tables and the touchstone on the cliff face. Those changes come pretty consistently when I ask to go to one place or the other so we Elizabeth Anns can all meet each together. This past year, it's been to the crystal room in the large cave in Ann's dimension. However, I'm never sure when I slap the touchstone and shout my mantra that I'll be sent to any other dimension. Even this morning, when I came to yours, Neil, I slapped the touchstone at the cliff s as usual and the next thing I knew, Ann and Beth were with me. It seems that shifts of dimensions are intentionally done. Whether by our animal familiars or some force from the Universal Counsel, your guess is as good as mine. The touchstone is a way out of any unknown dimension we're taken. We're able to turn around, slap the stone and shout our mantra and we return to our own dimension. It's a great relief to have that way back at those frightening moments."

"Is that how you all came here today? Was it planned by you or by your animal familiars? Reilly told me earlier to get up here and wait as you all would come to visit me today. Does that help you understand what happened, Liz?"

"Coming to your dimension this time was intentional. As I ran to the north cliffs, I decided to come back and talk with you. I wanted to make certain you had connected with Better's essence. However, this was the first time I've ever seen one of my others vanish from another dimension. When I'm home at the adjoined tables with Kip or when we're with the others in the crystal room, I hardly notice when one of the others comes or goes. Seeing Beth vanish from here was rather unnerving and I thought we would all go with her."

"It's different for me with Beth, Neil. The two of us have declared our love for each other and I see her so often in our cabins or the crystal room, that we've accepted it'll be this way for the rest of our lives. However, Beth's instant departure really shook you, didn't it, Neil?"

"Boy, I'll say it did. It took me back to that first time I saw her through the scope on my rifle. I thought she was my Mom. I got so excited, I held the rifle wrong and accidently pulled the trigger. When I ran to tell her I was sorry, I fell and the rifle shot again. That's when she disappeared. The next hour was horrible for me. I really thought I'd killed my own Mom. It made me so sick, I nearly killed myself."

"Oh no, Neil, I'm so glad you didn't. What stopped you?" Liz asks.

"I put the rifle up in my mouth and was pulling on the trigger when Mom was at the touchstone again. I guess that was when you came, Ann, and I thought you were my Mom. Remember? I shouted why she did she keep leaving and to come back here and stay with me. As I crossed this granite slab. I threw the rifle off to the side so I could hold on to her and keep her with me. For some reason the damned rifle went off again and you disappeared. That time, I decided you were just some sort of vision sent by my real Mom to stop me from killing myself."

"Well, I'm so glad you didn't do that and that something good came from Ann's appearance here. However, let's talk about what's happened since I talked to you about your mother. You told me about helping some Navy Seals capture several enemy soldiers. Have any more enemy come back to your beach?" Liz asks."

"Yeah, several came down from the mountains north of the cliffs, last week. Luckily, I was out on my beach deck eating some of those MRE's the Seals left me when Reilly began growling. I shushed him and looked to where twenty or more Chinese were coming out of the trees, shouting and yelling at each other. When Reilly and I heard that noise, I ran inside, grabbed the rifle and the rest of the food the Seals had left me. Reilly and me crawled under the deck to where I'd built a sort of fort when I was a kid. It was hidden so much, neither of my folks ever knew I'd put it there.

"We stayed there all day while those guys ransacked the house. When they finally walked down the beach, I could see each had changed into some of my Dad's clothes. Those guys were laughing and slapping each other on the back and a couple spoke English so I knew they intended to go south to look for food inside the other houses and business. Reilly and I watched from under the deck until we couldn't see or hear them anymore.

"That's when I pulled my cellphone out of my pocket and dialed 911. When a dispatcher in Hoquiam answered, I told her to contact the Captain of the Seals and tell him about there being more soldiers out on this beach. When I finished, the woman asked, 'Do you need any help". I hissed into the phone, 'Hell yes, lady, that's why I'm calling. I can't do much with a twenty-two target rifle. These bullets are only big enough to kill a rat.' She asked for my cell phone number and said she would pass my information on to the authorities. I thanked her said that would be great. She must have relayed my message immediately as the Captain of the same squad of Navy Seals called back and I told him what I'd seen from under my deck. Around midnight, someone rapped on the deck and Reilly and I came out from under the deck.

"Same as last time, one of the guys whispered, 'Son of a bitch, that's only a kid with his dog.' Again, all I saw was a wall of big black wetsuits. Then, the Captain stepped forward, asked my name and to repeat what I'd told him on the phone and what I'd said to the dispatch. Then, everyone relaxed and Reilly got a lot of petting from all those wet suited guys. The Captain asked if I would lead them to that path through the forest again and I did."

At this time, Neil stops as Reilly runs up to him and Liz snaps, "Don't stop, Neil. You've got to tell us what happened."

Smiling, the young man takes a deep breath and says, "Just like last time, those Seals surrounded each house, silently checked inside for the enemy. If they captured any, they tied them up and left them there. Within an hour, all the homes had been checked and those twenty

Chinese were captured without one shot being fired. When the Captain thanked me for my assistance, he told me I'd make a great Navy Seal and he'd be my mentor if I ever decided to try for the Naval Academy. I thanked him so much and told him that he was the first person I'd talked to since I came here with Reilly and found my parents dead. He didn't say a word but pulled me into a long hug. Isn't that something? I got hugged by a Captain of Navy Seals and when I let go of him... yeah, I hugged him back... the Captain told me I should expect several units of soldiers to come to the beach this week. They realize there must be more enemy soldiers in the mountains then they thought. He said at that time, he'd make sure that I got back to Portland where I can live safely again.

"That was a couple days ago. And I'm so glad that you ladies came today as I'll be probably be gone soon. When I told Mom, she said to expect it to happen soon. She was right. A jeep came this morning with a guy who had a letter for me. The letter said it's been arranged that I go back to my school as soon as I get back to Portland. The letter was from the Captain and he said he'd be sure that happens in the next week. The guy had a case of MRE's for me and a bag of kibble for Reilly. He really loves it."

Liz smiles through her tears and says, "That's wonderful, Neil. I'll bet you and Reilly are looking forward getting back to the rest of the world. I know your mother must be happy for you."

"She is and really pleased when I told her I knew what I want to do with my life. I'm going to go back to my school, get good grades and apply for the Naval Academy. After I graduate from that I'm going to become a Navy Seal. Those people were terrific and I want to be just like them. When I told them how I shot at you ladies by accident and even dropped my rifle, they all laughed and the Captain told me, 'A Navy Seal never drops his rifle.' And I said, 'I guess that's a really good thing, huh?' Everyone laughed at that, even the enemy soldier who spoke English."

When he says this the boy laughs heartily and the two women laugh with him. Smiling at the boy, Ann says, "I'm certain those people think you'll make a good Navy Seal. Especially once you're trained not drop your rifle or misfire it."

Neil laughs, "Yeah, thanks. It's a goal I've setup a plan for myself as it feels so right. I need discipline in my life since Mom and Dad aren't with me anymore. I hate that they're both gone and that I don't have anyone to be with. And, it was grand meeting the Navy Seals and it's been grand to have all of you here today. Mostly though, I know now that Mom is watching over me from wherever she is, out there, somewhere. Even if I don't see any of you again, I'll never forget the three of you. Thanks so much for coming here today and talking to me."

"We won't forget you either, Neil. Take care of yourself and keep your grades up. Hard work is the key. However, your folks would want you to enjoy your life, too. Remember that," Liz tells the boy and gives him a hug.

Then stepping across the granite slab, Liz says to the young man, "It's time Kip and I get back to our own dimension, Neil. The summer solstice is coming soon and, if past years are any indication of what will happen, I expect that our adjoined dimensions will open wider as its gets closer. Sit at the adjoined tables with your mother until you have to leave and maybe you'll come through to us at the adjoined tables. Take good care of Reilly and yourself. Come on, Kip. Let's get home."

"Wait for us, Liz," Ann says as she and Honey hurry to stand beside Liz and Kip at the cliff face. Turning, she says, "So long, Neil. Take care of you and Reilly. Most of all try to be happy."

Turning to Liz, she says, "Let's slap the touchstone and go home."

The two women raise their right hands and slap the golden stone as they shout, "I declare this run good and done."

# ELEVEN

## June 15th—Liz

**LIZ** and Kip appear in front of the golden touchstone in the cliff face and see hundreds of young people around the granite slab. Standing as still as a statue, Liz thinks,

*Kip? What the hell is going on? Have we gone into some other dimension?*

*No, dear one, this is the volley ball tryouts for the next summer's Olympics in Japan. The news has been saying this was going to happen today. The State is hosting the event here at our Redcliff's Beach. These young people are watching the first of the Olympic Team's volley ball tryouts. Get used to it as it's to last a whole two weeks. These are the young people who want to take part.*

Hardly breathing, Liz sees the young couple closest to her look right at her and she thinks,

*Kip, do something. They see us. If anyone screams I'm going to walk away and act normal. That man on the front end of this slab is the only one who keeps looking our way. Hey, isn't that Rudy? Turn and watch the game, Mister Sloan, you're bringing attention to us.*

*Lis, step over that girl and her buddy, then come directly to me.*

*Thanks, Rudy. I'll block the humans' thoughts, so they won't react to our being here. Go to the edge of the rock and hop onto the sand.*

*Good girl. Now come straight to me and I'll make certain there's a space for you.*

*Damn, how can I do that? This couple is all over each other. How can I move without, them screaming.*

*When I say go, step over their legs, move straight to the edge of the slab and step down to the sand. Go to the other side of Rudy and sit.*

Taking a deep breath, Liz does what Kip told her to do and steps off the rock and walks over and through a mass of splayed youths to sit next to Rudy Sloan. Without a word, Sloan nods and smiles. Liz does the same and for the next few minutes both watch the teams in front of them as if they care.

During this time, Kip lays down on the sand between his two humans' feet and the three heave sighs of relief. Turning to look at her charming neighbor, Liz says, "Howdy-doo, Mr. Sloan. How's your day going? Enjoying the game?"

Grinning back at her, Rudy points down the beach at the crowd of people watching matches at several volleyball courts along the six miles of beach. Hundreds more people perch on the high sand dunes that spread below Shoreline Drive or upon piles of float logs scattered amongst the dunes. Each group seems to cheering for one of the teams.

"Like what you see? That's going to be our view for the next full month. Aren't you thrilled?"

Liz whispers, "Wow, there must be a thousand people on our small strip of beach. How did these courts get set up so quickly? I was here before sunrise and didn't see any real activity. There were only the usual runners and groups of kids camping on the beach. Kip said theses courts are for the Olympic trials. Do they go down to the south cliffs?"

Then she sees Rudy's frowning nod and Liz chuckles, "So what's the score, old man of the sea? How are you doing?"

"With all these under thirty hormones smacking into each other, how do you think I've been doing? My butts more than a little numb and I feel like the last chaperone at a high school prom. Are you and Kip going home for the day? Good. I've already guessed that you two didn't remember today was the start of the month of tournaments. It's not even in full swing until this evening when they'll have the opening ceremony and fireworks down at the south cliffs. If you two had come back much later, you'd have caused quite a sensation. As is, you got back in time to enjoy the second round of games. Me? I'm leaving. I've sat on this soft springy granite slab since you slapped the stone and disappeared.

"You should know something my darling neighbor, I wasn't the only one who saw what happened to you. Several of the setup crew came down just as you did it and shouted about what they'd seen. When they saw me, they came over and asked if I'd seen that woman and her dog disappear. I looked surprised and said they must have imagined it as I hadn't seen anyone. When I said that those guys went back to marking out the courts, planting posts and attaching nets."

Smiling at him, Liz asks, "Are any of them still around here? I might get stopped and questioned. If I do, I'll say I've been here all morning. Truly, I've never seen this granite slab so well used. Where the hell are all their cars parked?"

"Everywhere and anywhere there isn't a private driveway. The cops are out in full force patrolling up and down so I don't think anyone's found our driveways. However, it's probably a good idea to get home and set out a couple sawhorses to block our lanes and check other things close to the road. I hope you remembered to lock your doors this morning."

Nodding, Liz looks down at Kip and thinks,

*What did you do to let us sneak over here without causing a commotion?*

Tilting his head to look up at her, Kip answers,

*I put a cloak of normalcy around us the moment we appeared.*

*Good boy. Now how about we get off this hard slab and go home. I really don't want to watch these games, do you?*

*Not at all. Let's go and check our house. After that, let's go over to Rudy's for lunch. Deal?*

*Deal.*

*If I'm going to make you lunch, do I get a say in this vote?*

Smiling, Liz says, "Oh, we'll bring the chow for all three of us. Deal?"

Rudy chuckles and answers, "Oh yes, indeed. That's a deal. I'm very interested to learn about what adventure you had today."

Slipping off the edge of the granite, Liz rubs her bottom and says, "How in the world did you sit there for four hours."

Lifting himself up on his good leg, Rudy balances at the waist high corner of the granite slab and says, "How, indeed. I did just what you are doing. I kept standing and cheering and rubbing my bum and pretending I was interested in the games. The least you can do it to take hold of my hand and walk me out to the edge of the waves so we look as if we're a real couple and not just two old farts."

Laughing, Liz takes his extended hand in hers and they follow Kip through the many volleyball fans spread out to the edge of the waves. Wading through the wash from the waves, the threesome start down the beach and Rudy begins to scold Liz and Kip, "Right now, I get to tell you both how much it scares me when you two disappear. It's was way past the time you usually get back to this dimension. I know as I've been keeping track of each of you disappearances and what amount of time they take. Damn it, Liz, I thought I'd have slap the stone myself and go bring you back. What happened?"

Surprised by his admonishment, Liz says, "I'm sorry we caused you concern, Rudy. We three Elizabeth Ann's happened to slap the stone the same second and went into Neil Gardner's dimension together. Then we had the loveliest long chat with the young man. Our animals came with us. It turned out they each knew Neil's dog, Reilly, in many other life times. Reilly was thrilled when he heard that you are living right next to Kip. All the animals want to gather together to see you. The sooner is better, they said, and to tell you hello for each of them. You can arrange that visit with Kip. You can come sit at the adjoined tables at my place. The animals come together over the golden stone often. I'd love to see how they'll greet you after so many lifetimes."

"Hey, what a great idea. Kip? Tell them I'll make sure I'm there to greet them. Okay?"

*Sounds good to me, Rudy. They sure love you. Especially Reilly.*

"Is that why you were gone so long a time?"

"No, not really. When we saw Neil was without his rifle and waiting on the same corner of the granite slab you sat on all morning, we Parallel Lives had so many questions about his life that Neil took time to answer them all. It was such a lovely time that we forgot how long we'd been there. It wasn't until Beth and Dandy vanished practically in mid-sentence that Ann and I knew we needed to go, also.

As the couple walk down the edge of the waves, Liz tell Rudy what Neil had shared with them. When she told about the Chinese attacking their country, Rudy was shocked and demanded to know all Neil had told them. When they reach the flag pole marking the path through the sand dunes to her house, Liz stops and says, "It was so nice to talk with that young man about his life, I hated to leave him and Reilly. Of course, that dog is his familiar and has talked to Neil ever since the boy got him as a puppy. Reilly was so glad to see so many of his old friends, wasn't he, Kip?"

*Yes, and it was great to see him as well. The two of us had three lifetimes together and a lot to catch up on. While the humans talked, we chased each other up and down the beach. When Liz said it was time for us to go, Reilly said to tell you Hi and to meet us at the golden stone in Liz's home. He also wondered if you'll be coming with Liz and me to the crystal room on the Summer Solstice. Everyone connected to the original Elizabeth Ann is to come to the crystal room before sunrise on that morning...*

*I sure will be, Kip. The Universal Counsel contacted me last week. Tell the familiars we'll meet at the golden stone in Liz's home before then. It'll be good to see Reilly and the others again. He's such a great choice for that kid to have as a companion at this time of his life, especially now that his parents are gone. Reilly was my buddy years ago in Egypt and twice in what they now call ancient Rome. Once before and one after, Caesar's time. Liz? Has Kip told you that I was with Julius as his speech writer during one of my very first lives? Good old Reilly was my dog at that time and what a great friend he was. Nearly as great as you've been to Liz in this life, Kip. Since Neil's life has changed so radically, Reilly will make sure the boy stays on track.*

Okay, Rudy, let me get this straight, you and Kip have had many lifetimes together and you've had many with Reilly as well? Is that why we all went through to Neil's dimension this morning?

Though she is asking Rudy, it is Kip who answers tersely,

*Of course, it is, you ninny. Each of the Elizabeth Anns needed to finalize the connection you made with Bette and her son, Neil. She was the reason Beth and Ann were sent into that dimension that first day. Of course, you will see Bette Ann's essence in the crystal room on the Summer Solstice and Reilly will bring Neil. That way, we can say goodbye to Bette Ann and the others leaving with Jill and James Anderson at that time. You will enjoy your meeting with your parents before deciding whether to go with them or return to your own dimensions and live out your lives. You need to give this some thought, missy.*

Suddenly, Rudy seems to be choking and covers his mouth. Concerned, Liz asks, "Are you all right?"

Laughing aloud, he nods looking into her eyes and she sees tears roll down his cheeks. Thinking it had to be something she said, Liz raises her eyebrows and shrugs her shoulders, saying, "Whhaattt?"

Taking a deep breath, Rudy smiles at her before he answers, "Oh nothing really, dear heart. I just get tickled by how you and Kip banter back and forth with each other."

Looking into his face, Kip asks,

*Okay, Mr. Sloan, enough of that. You haven't really told us what you were doing at the cliffs at this time of the morning? Don't tell us you keep track of our disappearances or simply like beach volleyball. You told me when you read in the newspaper about our beach being selected that it had to be the silliest sport.*

*Oh, ho, ho, ho, my old friend. Sometimes you can be such a smarty-pants. Can't you believe that I missed you and your beautiful mistress? I waited for you both so I could walk you both back home?*

*Hey, you two, I'm right here and can hear everything you say to each other. However, I'll keep silent as I'm loving the things you're both saying about me. Go ahead, amuse yourselves.*

*We've said enough, spoiled one. Rather, you said enough, Mr. Sloan. We're back home, so when we come over with lunch, I expect you to get my tennis ball from under the sofa and toss it into the waves for me. Liz, when you fix lunch,* could you bring my kibble, too? Hey, Rudy, where did you have that red tennis ball? Is it new? Can you throw it out to that biggest wave? Huh? Huh?

Laughing, Rudy looks first at Liz, then down at Kip and says aloud, "Okay, I give up. With both of you is thinking over the other, I'm not sure who said what. So here's the deal. I'll assume it was Kip who wants me to throw this new tennis ball I brought to the cliffs. However, from now on, Liz, would you please look into my eyes with your big blue ones and speak to me with that sultry voice of yours. That way I won't make a fool of myself and say something meant for Liz to Kip. Does that sound like a good idea?"

Liz smiles at the charming man and says, "I don't know about doing that. For one thing, I just love getting into you head, Mr. Sloan. One question, how did you know we were back in our dimension? Was it Kip or me?"

"You should know by now, me little beauty, I'm tuned into your vibes. However, Kip's thoughts take priority over both of ours. Before you ask, I don't know why that is. It is the way the Universal Council power given to the animal familiars' works. Probably for our safety and comfort."

Staring at Rudy and then Kip, Liz sighs and says, "I don't think I'll ever get used to having my darling dog be such an important entity within the Universe. Why couldn't you just be a normal loving animal friend, Kip? What will I do if that Universal Council decides it's time for you to go elsewhere and take you from me?"

*I'll be with you for as long as you need me, darling Liz. Do not despair. The time for me to leave is far into the future and you'll be an old, old, woman long before I am called to another dimension. Now, old man, throw that ball out to the waves. We're home.*

Tossing the new red tennis ball, Rudy watches the dog run into the waves and grab the bobbing ball off the rush of waves. Turning towards his two humans, the large dog races back to Rudy and drops the ball at the man's feet. However, the couple is deep into their own conversation and not paying attention. Seeing a group of children tossing a Frisbee, Kip drops the ball and races to join their game.

Fascinated by the man beside her, Liz walks to the flag pole and sits down on the soft sand beside it. Patting the sand beside her, she says, "Plant your sore butt right here, Mr. Sloan and tell me who really sent you to live here at Redcliff's Beach in the house next to mine. Huh? I'd really like to understand what I'm up against and why I'm so blessed to have both Kip and you in my life. Would you explain yourself, Mister Sloan?"

"You were chosen when Peter's essence returned and you accepted that he was within a beam of light which came from no earthly light source. You shouted at him to go away only once. After those first moments, you settled down and listened to what he had to tell you about himself and your life. When the two essences appeared with him, you accepted they belonged to your Parallel Lives. You quickly understood how and why Beth and Eliza were connected to you and you patiently explained these things to them until they understood what you said was true."

"Yes, I remember doing that. But don't other people have their deceased loved ones return to them as Peter did to me."

"Yes, it happens very often. However, not many humans recognize their loved one's soul as something good. Those left become frightened of their loved one's image and they close their minds to whatever that essence wanted to share with them. Few living understand that the dead return only to tell their loved ones good things, never to do evil. These entities come to ease the pain caused by their deaths."

"I have to say that Peter's appearance within the beam of light frightened me at first. Then, it was just so wonderful to see him as the youth he'd been when we first met. When I heard his wonderful voice and rejoiced in each of his words. After our trip back through our years together, he told me the Universal Council needed to send his essence elsewhere. I understood then that our souls move from one life to the next, letting our essences live one life after another, for all time."

"Ah, Liz, you're truly a magical being. Listen how easily you tell about that time and what you've now come to believe. If anyone heard you, they would rejoice and let go of their fear of death. Have you shared your thoughts with others?"

"Not really, Rudy. Not even with Kip. After he came, he told me so much about his life, I figured he already knew more than I did about mine. Besides, I'd come to those realizations because of Peter. I've been afraid others would scoff at me or even try to make more of me than I am. I did share my experience with Peter to the three Elizabeth Ann's that first month of June two years ago, but only because they had their own experiences with their loved ones. As I say this, I realize that was before Ann or her sister, Dana, came into our lives. Eliza was the last to be convinced that we Parallel Lives came from the one original child named Elizabeth Ann Andersons. Now, we each accepted that child is our own Beth Anderson."

"Eliza's been gone a year this Solstice, Liz. Ann is a different person. She was a child when she discovered the crystal room. Since then, she has been its protector ever since. Remember how badly you and Beth felt when you understood that she hadn't shared the crystal room with you and Beth? Tell Ann about the true spiritual importance of the Parallel Lives of Elizabeth Ann or make certain Beth has shared those things with Ann and that she truly understands."

"I will, Rudy. However, I'm almost positive that Beth said she discussed everything with Ann when they first met. After all, they love each other in the deepest way possible. They must have shared everything about their lives. When I first met Ann, she knew everything about Eliza and me. When she came through to the adjoined tables, she was ready to be a part of our lives. However, if it will make you happy, I'll ask Beth if Ann understands everything about this."

Watching Liz come to her own conclusion, Rudy smiles and wraps both arms around her, kisses both her cheeks and forehead. Then as he nuzzles her right ear, he whispers, "Ah darling Liz, you are a dear soul. I do believe I love you more than life itself. In fact, I know I do. Remember I said I wouldn't ask for us to be together for at least six months. Well, my dear sweetest soul, would you be so inclined to ponder on my whole-hearted proposal of marriage? I would happily kneel down in front of you here and now, or at some time in the near future, to pop the question."

Pulling back to look into his handsome face, Liz says softly, "Ah Rudy, you dear, darling soul, I would truly consider that question coming from you at any date to be the most wonderful invitation to marriage that anyone could be blessed to hear. I also believe that the six month time frame put on you when we first met was one of the most ridiculous things I could ever have done."

Almost instantly, Liz feels the nudge of a wet nose on her bare knees and realizes that Kip is sitting on the sand in front of them. Before either human can say a word, they hear,

*Must you two neck on a public beach? Mary and Larry's grandkids have stopped tossing the Frisbee for me and are staring, giggling and pointing at the two old kissy-face folks on the sand dune. I must say, I am very pleased to see my old folks were their old folks. Does this public display of lust mean something more than just old folk's fun in the sun?*

Reaching out to pull the large dog into a rough hug, Rudy ruffles Kips thick fur and says, "Yes, old friend. It means that your old folks are getting very inclined to join together under one roof so that we can both keep a close eye on our dearest familiar named Kip. Would you be so inclined to be agreeable to such an arrangement? Hmmm?"

*Yeah, yeah, yeah.*

# TWELVE

## June 15<sup>th</sup>—Beth

**BETH** and Dandy are instantly transported from Neil Gardner's dimension to the middle of the crystal room. Stunned by the unexpected change of dimensions, Beth says to Dandy, "Well kiddo, looks as if the Universe wanted us in the crystal room. That's good, as it's where I wanted to come to in the first place. Let's go out to the clifftops and see if Ann and Honey are back yet. Stay close to me. Remember, seagulls think kitties are a prime food source."

As she starts towards the stairs up to the opening in the cave's ceiling, the large cat runs ahead of her and stands on the bottom step and Beth hears,

*Stop right there. Don't come any closer to the stairs. You are to stay here with me. I have been told to take you to the crystal thrones and you are to sit on the first throne where you are to meditate. You will receive the last message from the Universal Council at this time. Yes, it is a week before the Summer Solstice. However, this information you will prepare you for that special day. Then you will go to the adjoined table where the other Elizabeth Anns will gather. At that time you three will lay your hands upon the golden bowl and sit with your bare feet on the stone under the tables. It is then when each of you will receive the directions needed for you to prepare yourselves for that special day.*

Surprised that her cat has spoken to her with such authority, Beth frowns at the cat and says, "Dandy? The way you said that is almost scary to me. Have you always been so involved in directing me to receive the messages from the stone these past two years? Were you animal familiars the reason we went into Neil Gardner's dimension?"

*As your animal familiar, I am to lead you only when it is needed for you to make the right choice. This is the same for all animal familiars. Right now, your instructions are simple. Cross the fire-tiles and go up the stairs to the crystal thrones. Sit upon the first throne. Close your eyes and relax. The meditation will begin instantly. I am to sit on your lap as you receive instructions from the Universal Council. I will purr loudly to let you know you are safe and I am with you.*

Picking up the large cat, Beth climbs the stairs and sits upon the first beautifully sculpted crystal throne. Placing Dandy on her lap, Beth folds her arms around the animal, closes her eyes and leans back against the glittering stone. Instantly, images of crowds of cheering people fill the massive room and her mind. Each person, man and woman, holds a long golden staff high over their head and soon the cheers become a deafening roar of thousands of souls within and over the hillsides.

Turning to her left, she sees a handsome dark haired man sitting straight-backed on the larger throne. This man is the same who greeted her Nordic ship when she first arrived at this Port of the Chosen Ones. He is the very same man who joined her in matrimony and took her virginity with a wild and passionate copulation that evening.

Next to her, between the two large thrones, is a wide jeweled bench. Upon this bench are two small children, both girls. The oldest is a dark haired dark eyed four year old. The younger is a two year old with the same white hair and blue eyes as her mother. Both children wear dresses of spun gold and silver threads with brilliant jewels woven into the fabric. Wrapping each small head is a golden band covered with emeralds.

As the crowd shouts their greeting to the family, the older child stands upon the bench and waves to the people. This causes the crowd to roar with their approval. Excited by their reaction, the child twirls around to show off her beautiful dress and, at the same time, looks up to see the large crystal formation hanging over her head, from the cave's ceiling. Clapping her hands, the child stands on her tiptoes and tries to touch the larger crystal hanging out of reach high over her head. As she does, the crowd begins to chant, "Lift her high. Lift her high." It is then that the dark handsome man beside her stands, picks up this child and lifts her up to the crystal formation as if to let her pick an apple off a tree.

When she is lifted to the largest crystal, the small dark haired beauty slaps the crystal which causes it to ring out with the purest of tone. Again, the crowd erupts with cheers. Inspired by these cheering people before her, the youngest child crawls upon her side of the bench and dances to the tempo of her sisters crystal tones, Flapping her small arms as if trying to take flight, she turns her head up to the crystal formation and crows loudly as if a rooster.

When she sees the child do this, Beth knows for certain that in some past life, she did the very same thing, years and years ago. In this flash of certainty, Beth knows she was this younger child, eons ago. The unexpected knowledge stuns her and she stares at the images until she falls into a deep trance. When this happens, she hears Dandelion's deep purr turn into a rolling roar which causes the crystal formations to vibrate harmoniously.

In this instant, her soul's essence leaves her body and soars out through the opening in the ceiling of the crystal room. Freed at last, it flashes straight to the edge of the Universe where a vast golden void spreads out far beyond the last galaxy. Staring into this golden space, Beth asks, "Why am I here? What am I to see? Is this what I'm to share with my others? Am I to throw myself into the abyss beyond?"

As an answer, several shooting stars flash past her to vanish into the shimmering void. When she can no longer sees their sparkling comet tail debris, Beth asks again, "Am I follow those comets into the abyss? Please, tell me, why am I here? What do I do with this knowledge now? Am I to step into this golden void of nothingness?"

*Of course not, silly. I brought you to the edge of time. Few see it before their death. It's only after death, when you are able to go to the edge of this abyss. I show you this only so you will know the truth about life and what the Universe belongs to as a whole. Study the abyss only with your eyes. There will be a time in the near future for you to know all there is to know. When that comes, you will pass through the golden shroud and rejoice for you will have reached your highest lifetime.*

At this moment, Beth sees her large orange cat change into a full sized orange and black striped tiger. When this happens, the cat's purr changes into a vibrating rumble and Beth nuzzles her face into the animal's thick fur. Leaning against the animal's left side, she wraps her arm over the animal's back and murmurs, "I love you, darling Dandy. You are so beautiful."

The large beautiful animal turns its head and Beth sees brilliant golden flecks of light flash through its slanted green eyes and hears,

*Be not afraid, dear one, for I am with you. You are anointed with the blessings of our Master of all the Universe who lives beyond the shimmering golden light. Those who come this way are at the end of their highest life, the very last and this is why I have brought you here.*

Shivering with joy as his words fill her being, Beth whispers, "Oh my darling Dandelion, I always knew you were more than the cathouse you showed me. I'm thrilled to see you as you truly are. Thank you for showing me this beautiful space. I am so grateful to have had you in my life. Am I to tell the other Elizabeth Anns about what I've been shown?"

*No, dear one, this viewing is for your knowledge. Other Parallel Lives of Elizabeth Ann will learn of this when they reach their own highest levels of life. Those you know have more to before their lives run its course. Now silence your mind and let the rapture of being here fill your being as it surrounds us both. Once you have felt his ecstasy, you will return to the crystal room on Ann's Redcliff's Beach for she has now come home.*

As Dandelion speaks, Beth sees several million galaxies within the Universe and she turns one last time towards the shimmering golden void. Immediately she is filled with all the passion she had experienced in each life and her body pulses with explosive urges of a thousand lifetimes. Clinging to the massive tiger's thick fur, she screams out with each orgasmic release rushes through her. Each time she does, the large massive tiger roars out its own erotic pleasure of returning once more to the edge of the Universe.

Unable to hold onto Dandelion any longer, Beth releases her hold on him and soars into the vast golden void to come face to face with the entity that gave life and meaning to all things. Whispering to this entity, Beth says, "Thank you, for Dandy. Thank you giving my many lives and thank you for being here for us all."

It is those words which send Beth into the crystal room and she wakens to find herself sitting upon the crystal throne. For several seconds, her body pulses with left over pleasures and she tries to clear her vision by blinking her eyes. Finally, two blurry shapes form in front of her and Beth sees Ann standing in front of the thrones. Honey, her Golden Retriever is standing to Ann's left and both are staring up at the crystal throne.

In that first moment, Beth sees Ann's bright blue eyes and swells with the loves she has for this Elizabeth Ann Anderson. Remembering the shimmering golden void at the edge of the Universe, Beth knows for certain that she wants to share some of what she saw. However, as she begins to speak, Beth hears,

*Darling Dandelion, we are very happy you decided to bring our original Elizabeth Ann Anderson back to be with us for the time we have left. Come down here with us and let's spend this day together.*

*I needed to show her the shimmering void and how much is there that she will soon experience. Honey, tell your mistress she will not see what Beth has seen for several lifetimes. Therefore, what I am saying is entering only your ears. And you must not let Ann know where I took Beth. The Universal Council intends for us familiars to leave our animals familiars this lifetime. We are needed for other lives which need our attention. If you wish to do so, each animal may stay with their mistress if they desire to do so. Know that if you do, neither human nor animal left by the familiars will remember any of their magic when this happens.*

"Hey, you two. Talk so that Ann and I can hear you. I only heard something about the Universal Council sending you on to other lives? When is this supposed to happen?"

Ann says, "Yikes. They can't take Honey from me. She's my dog and I love her. Damn it, I won't have it. I love my dog and I want to keep her for as long as she lives."

*Don't worry, loved one, I won't be going anywhere. I'm your dog for all my life. It's this damned familiar that's borrowed my body this past year that will leave us. I'll be here for as long as I'm alive and to help you through the final days of being a Parallel Life of Elizabeth Ann Anderson.*

*Honey is right, Ann. I'll make certain she stays here with you after the Solstice.*

Still sitting on the crystal throne, Beth looks down at Dandy and asks, "Will that be the same for you, Dandy? I don't want to give you up to someone I don't even know. Dandy? Will you have to go if the Universal Council calls you to go away?"

*I'll never leave you, dear one. I'm your cat for all the time you have in this lifetime. That's the truth, dear one.*

Looking down at Ann, Beth asks, "Ann? What are you going to do for the rest of the day? I'd like to visit with you for a while, if you and Honey have time."

"That'd be great. I tell you, Beth, it really shook me when you and Dandy vanished from Neil's dimension without saying a word to me."

"Did you stay long after I left?" Beth asks.

"Only a few minutes. Liz and Kip needed to leave and we went at the same time they did. I doubt we'll see Neil again. He doesn't need us anymore. His connection with his mother and the Captain of the Navy Seals has given him the courage to take control of his future. It was so good to see that he's decided what sort of man he wants to become. So few kids do that at that age. Bette must be so proud of him. I hope she'll be in the crystal room on the Solstice and see her as we did Eliza's essence last year."

# THIRTEEN

*June 15th—Ann*

ANN watches Beth and Dandy come down from the crystal thrones and stands in front of her before she says, "Did the thrones give you any messages that you're to share from your meditation? Or should I ask?"

Smiling at Ann, Beth says, "Oh, Ann. It was magical. Really beautiful. Dandelion took me back to when I first saw the crystal cave when a man and I were joined together for our world and others in the Universe to unit. This time, there were two small children with us. I felt the youngest was me as she looked just like the two of us had with white hair and big blue eyes. The other looked exactly as Dana Marie had when she was small. After that, Dandy took me somewhere amazing. It was there that Dandy became a magnificent Siberian Tiger. I wasn't surprised as I always knew she was more than a house cat. Aren't you, my darling kitty?"

*I am that for as long as we both shall live.*

It's then that Beth places the orange cat down on the fire-opal tiled floor of the crystal room. Smiling, Ann takes Beth's hand and says, "We've each had quite a day, that's for sure. Going into Neil Gardner's dimension again was rather traumatizing for me. However, it was amazing to have all three of us there at the same time was wonderful. When Honey and I got back here, I wasn't surprised to see you meditating on the throne. You looked so regal and seemed to glow."

Smiling sweetly at Ann, Beth says, "Yes, my dear, I know I did. After all, I am the original Elizabeth Ann Anderson. Is this the same day we were in Neil's dimension? I feel as if I've been on a very long trip and am exhausted. Would you forgive me if I changed my mind and went to my own home? I really need to lay down and have a good nap."

"Of course, darling, go have a good rest. I'll come to you later and fix dinner for both of us. While we're eating, at the adjoined tables, maybe Liz and Kip will join us there. Honey and I are going out to the cliff top kitchen to meet Dana in a few minutes. She called and said she has a big surprise for me. I'll let you know what it is when I see you later. Love you, darling. Have a good snooze."

"Will do. Thanks." Beth says as the two give kisses and hug each other. "See you later, darling. Tell Dana Hello for me," In the next second, Beth and Dandy vanish from the crystal room and though Ann knew Beth was going, the sudden disappearance of the women she loves leaves Ann a bit undone.

Walking quickly up the stairs to the opening to the outside, she says, "You know what, Honey? I don't think I'll ever get used to the goings and comings we Elizabeth Ann's do. It really takes my breath away. Does it bother you?"

*Not at all, dear one. You must remember that I've had eons to get used to the comings and goings of thousands of entities within the Universes. Isn't that Dana down there, shouting at you?*

From the top of the steep berm around the opening in the caves roof, Ann sees her sister at the table in the cliff top kitchen. Hurrying down the path to where Dana waits, Ann gives a pleased shout, "I'm so glad you're here. I'm dying of curiosity. What is this big surprise you have? Did another museum buy another painting for a zillion dollars?"

"Don't I wish? Nope, not today. This time it's something wonderfully personal. I told Cliff I had to tell you first, before we announced it for all to know. In fact, I'm surprised you haven't guessed our secret by now. Okay, here goes. Look at my left hand. See anything bright and shiny? Yes, darling Ann, I said yes to my darling. Sheriff Cliff Deaton popped the big question, again, right after our tussle with the neighbor boys and the gasoline. This time, I said yes."

"What do you mean he finally popped the question? How long have you two known each other? That is more than to say Hello?"

"For two years, darling sister, Cliff and I've met three years ago and been serious for the last two of those."

"What? When did you ever get together? No, that's not what I meant to say. Darling, I'm happy you're happy. Yes, I am, truly, for you both. However, when I kept telling you how perfect he was for you, you seemed so disinterested. How and why did you hide this from everyone? I've not heard one peep of gossip about the two of you. How did you ever do that? When will the big day happen?"

"Wait, Ann, stop. Let me answer you. The answer to your most important question is this coming Saturday at Hoquiam's Shilo Inn in their Skylight Room. Cliff's brother is a minister and will officiate for us. We got the license yesterday right before we rented the room at the Shilo. We hired the band playing there at night and their chef will cater the food. We're not sending invitations as the time's too short. So Cliff wrote up and placed a full page ad in the three regional papers which will run the next three days. It invites everyone who cares about us to come. We spent last night calling out of towners. Tonight we'll call most of our friends in the area. The ads are because Cliff doesn't want to leave out anyone who might have voted for him and wants to come celebrate with us. Will you be my Maid of Honor and stand up with me?"

"Me? Oh, yes, of course, I will, darling. I can't think of anything I'd like better. That is, if I don't have to wear a hot pink satin shift, I will. What are you planning to wear?"

"Definitely not white. I lost that opportunity years ago. I'm wearing that beautiful purple silk Vera Wang I bought for my opening at the MOMA in New York last year. It fits great and Cliff thinks it's perfect. He'll wear the dark grey Armani silk suit he got for the same opening.

To top it off, he'll us the same Salvador Dali tie I gave to him at that time. It's a crazy bold print that goes perfectly with my dress. I must say, we looked absolutely smashing at that show's opening. I expect the locals here will do a lot of oohing and aahing over the look but it's our wedding and that's what we want to wear. Do you think that'll be too obnoxious for a wedding?"

"You'll both look absolutely beautiful and that's the most important thing at any wedding. Why did you keep your relationship with Cliff a secret from me for so long? That New York opening was the one I didn't get to as I had the flu. If I'd been there, would you two have told me then that you were involved? Good. Then I won't feel slighted though I do feel a bit like an idiot that I kept pointing you in his direction and you never gave yourself away. Truly, how dense am I to not have realized you two were already involved? What was the reason for keeping the secret for so long? Is there an ex-wife?"

"Nope. We first met at the opening of my gallery in Ocean Shores and it was the year he was first elected Sheriff. We soon realized we were into more than a causal relationship and decided to keep the nosey-posies out of our lives. We used designated phones and saw each other out of town. Our get-aways were so much fun and no one ever connected us together. We met at the first preplanned location, we would plan for the next and never went to the same place twice. Last week, during the arson scare, you kept telling me how perfect he'd be for me, it was so hard not to tell you that you were right. When I took Cliff into your office to write out my statement, I told him what you'd said and that it was time to tell you."

"It that the reason he popped the question?"

"Yes and told me it was the last time he'd ask. That arson attempt scared the hell out of both of us and I said 'Yes'. Which reminds me, darling Ann, I will not be moving up here or taking over half of your holdings. My involvement with Cliff has been the only reason I hesitated to let you change the land titles. This place is yours and always should only belong to you."

"The point of land where the cabin sits belonged to Dad and he'd want us both to share that place. So no matter what you say, that cabin is yours as well as mine. After all, dear sister, our folks would want it that way."

"Okay, I'd love to share the cabin with you. But the rest is yours and that's all I'll say on the matter. Remember, it was you who found the cave and the crystal room when we were children. It was you who protected it all these years. You were the one who bought miles of cliff tops and built your home on the hillside so you could oversee the crystal room. It was you that rediscovered the golden stone within the piece of cement floor was still on that largest sea stack. It was you who built the new cabin over it. I thank you for doing that and for offering me a place to call home in my old age. However, in a few days, I will marry Cliff Deaton and, as Dana Deaton, I will be mistress of Cliff's new home in Hoquiam which I helped him find."

"I'm sure you'll have a wonderful life, darling. I have no doubts that you and Cliff will be very happy together. Cliff is one of the loveliest men I've ever met and I'll be proud to have him as a brother-in-law."

"Thank you for saying that, Ann. Since we are being so honest with each other, I must tell you this, also. I don't want to be part of your Summer Solstice. Whatever is to happen in the crystal room on that day is for you Elizabeths. I'm sorry. That crystal room give me the willies. I just don't feel the excitement about it as you Elizabeth Anns do. I love your cliff top kitchen area and the cabin. Being here on the bench with the stone wall behind us, high above the ocean, is totally amazing to me. Whenever I come to this amazing spot and breathe this wonderful ocean air, I am renewed. The peace, the quiet, the surrounding serenity are exactly what I longed for all those years I was away. This is the place for me, here on top of these beautiful cliffs overlooking the Pacific Ocean and all her many moods."

"Dana, darling, always do what you feel is right for you. With your wedding planned for this Saturday, by the Summer Solstice next week, you will be an old married lady and on your honeymoon. Thank you so much for being so honest and for including me in your ceremony. I love you, my beautiful sister, and want you to be happy."

"Thank you for understanding and agreeing to stand up with me, Ann. My wedding wouldn't be the same without you." Dana says to Ann as they hug.

As the sisters turn back to their lunch, Ann feels a cold nose on her bare calf and hears,

*All right, all right. Get on with telling Dana about Neil Gardner. Just don't tell her about hearing me talk to you. She would never sit by me again. Understand?*

Honey's words cause Ann to choke on a bite of food and she starts coughing. Quickly standing, she walks to the edge of the cliffs and spits the bite out of her mouth. Suddenly, Dana rushes to Ann's side and pulls her back towards the table and pounds on Ann's back.

Twisting away, Ann frowns at her sister and sputters, "Stop, Dana. Don't pull … I just spit… over the edge… couldn't swallow. Whew… Okay, I'm okay, now… really. Just talked with a mouth full of food… and choked on a bit of it. Whew… I hate when that happens, don't you?"

"Especially when someone pounds on me. I'm sorry, darling, but when you moved so suddenly to the edge of the cliffs, it scared me. I thought you were going to fall off the cliff. Can you talk now? Good. How about telling me about Neil Gardner? I have to meet Cliff in an hour at the Shilo."

"Yes, I nearly forgot." Ann smiles at her sister and begins, "Honey and I went into Neil's dimension this morning at the same second as Beth and Liz. Our animal familiars came with us and knew Neil's dog Reilly. When I first saw I was back in that boy's dimension, it scared me and I stayed behind the others. This time, the kid had changed and being with everyone else put us all at ease. Now, looking back, I realize what a great times we all had in his dimension.

"Neil didn't have his rifle with him as the government placed a squad of soldier in the area to take pick up any Chinese that wander down from the mountains. Once he got over our sudden appearance, he was as excited to see the three of us as we were to see him. As it did that first time, the young man was a bit overcome by our resemblance to his mother, Bette Gardner. When we finally got to talking to him, he welcomed all three of us by name, shook our hands and apologized for shooting at us before. Then, he thanked Liz for bringing us with her and telling him his mother's message to meet with him at the golden stone in the floor of the cabin area of their home. It was a wonderful time for all of us."

"Was that the first time you Elizabeths have been together in another dimension besides at the adjoined tables and the crystal cave?"

"Why…yes, now that you ask, it was. I wonder if Liz or Beth have any thoughts about that fact. Yes and it was the first time our animal familiars came with us. Funny how natural that seemed, so easy and normal…."

For the next hour, Ann shares her experiences with her others in Neil Gardner's dimension and finally concludes, "Just as she said that to Neil, Beth and Dandy vanished from the granite slab. Poof. Not saying a word to anyone. It was so unexpected that it really shook me."

Dana says, "Good. It always rattles me and I'm relieved to hear that it shook you too. Now you know how I feel when you disappear."

As she says this, Dana's cell phone rings and she answers with, "Oh, yes darling, I'll meet you there. I'm just finishing lunch with Ann. Yes, I told her and she's thrill and agreed to be my Maid of Honor. What time did you say the appointment was? Okay, I'll see you in a half hour. Bye."

Standing, Dana moves to Beth and gives her a quick hug, saying, "I'm off. Cliff and his brother are at the Shilo Inn. I'm have an appointment with the florist in a half hour and then we'll both sample food Shilo's Chef plans to cater for our wedding. I thought that was to be later this afternoon… Love you, sis. I'll give you a call when we're done. Is there anything else you want to tell me about Neil?"

"Not now, dear. I'm going up to the house as soon as I clean up the picnic. I'll take you basket up to the house. Go, meet Cliff at the Shilo. We'll talk later about what I will wear. I have three lovely choices and you can help me decide which one to wear. Okay?"

"Just not white, black or purple. Those colors aren't up for grabs."

"Nope, it's either teal green or deep rose. I'm leaning toward the rose."

"Great choice. I love that dress. You'll make us look as if we planned this thing months ago. I'll call you later."

"Give Cliff a hug for me"

Watching Dana run down the path from the clifftops, Ann smiles when her sister stops at the junction of the trail up to the house, turns and waves. Waving back, Ann feels a sense of relief and thinks,

*Am I glad she's not going to the crystal room for the Solstice or that she's getting married or that she's not taking up my offer for half of all I've worked so hard to do on this beach? What do you think it is, Honey?*

*It is all of those, dear heart. Mostly though, it is that Dana doesn't want to come with us on the Solstice. Doesn't that one fit perfectly into your feelings?*

*Yes. That's right. Here all this time, I thought since she knew about Parallel Lives that she should be part of what we go through. Now I see I was wrong. Whatever the Parallel Lives of Elizabeth Ann do, at any time, is truly for us alone.*

*Remember the accident which split you Elizabeths from the original child was very deadly to each family in some way. Though your family survived, other Elizabeths lost at least one or all of their family. Those deaths happened long ago and those entities have already gone on to other lives.*

# FOURTEEN

*June 20th—The Summer Solstice*

*Liz*

**LIZ and Kip** run to the north cliffs while stars still shine brightly in the eastern sky. "We did it, Kip, we're here long before the glow of sunrise comes over the mountains. This is just as you said we must do. Are the others around us? Are they already in the crystal room? I hope they are."

*Stop worrying about them. Slap that stone and say your mantra. We're to meet Rudy Sloan in the crystal room when we get there. Do it. Now.*

Shocked by the dog's demands, Liz frowns at the animal and says, "Hey kiddo, take it easy. That sun won't crack over the tops for an hour. Be nice or I'll send you home."

*You don't control me, Liz. Not anymore. Slap your touchstone and shout your mantra. Don't you want to see who's waiting for you?*

Without answering, Liz slaps the stone and shouts, "This run is good and done." Instantly, both she and Kip are standing on the fire-opal tiled floor of the crystal room and she shouts, "Kip, we're here."

The shout causes crystal groupings to ring softly for several seconds and, as this happens, a large black hole opens in the fire-opal tiles at the base of the crystal thrones. Watching the hole widen until it is halfway across the room, Liz pulls Kip over to her leg and asks, "Should this be happening? That hole seems a lot bigger than the one last year."

*It's the same, dear one. It's called a wormhole and carries entities from one area in space to wherever they want to go. It can move users millions of miles in split seconds. This is how your parents, James and Jill Anderson, came to talk to you Elizabeth Anns last Summer Solstice. They are using it for the same this year. No harm will come to you. Watch and rejoice at what is going to happen.*

"I don't understand, Kip. Beth and Ann are coming, aren't they?"

*You Elizabeth Anns are to experience your own meeting with your parents without the intrusion of others. Each of their familiars are talking to them as I am doing with you. Each of you face different futures and must know your destiny is yours alone. You have been separated from each other on this Summer Solstice to live the life you were destined for within your own dimension.*

Suddenly, a golden staircase rises up to the tops of the large black hole and fills the dark void until it is level with the fire-opal tiles of the crystal room's floor. Then the two surfaces meld together and the fire-opals around the staircase's diameter gleam brilliantly. Without realizing that she does so, Liz begins to pant rapidly and hears,

*Calm yourself, dear one. Let your eyes wander about the room. Study the perfection of each magnificent crystal formation. Think of nothing. Let your mind be filled with the beauty before you. Count each crystal until there are no more numbers. You will find their total is more than the stars in the heavens.*

Doing as she is told, Liz forces herself to breathe slowly as she looks at each formation flashing within the magnificent cave room. Without realizing it, she soon falls into a trance. Becoming very still, her arms hang at her sides with her palms facing outwards. A pleasant smile settles across her lips and her pure blue eyes open wide as she stares at her surroundings. Slowly, she becomes aware of the group of people who have appeared at the top of the golden stairway and move towards her.

She recognizes each of them for who they are and says, "Mother. Father. Dana Marie. Aunt Margaret. How wonderful to see you all here. Please, come and stand in front of me. This is my animal familiar, Kip. He is my good friend and my protector. We welcome you to our crystal room on this Summer Solstice. I've missed you so much my dear parents, Jill and James Anderson. It's been too long since you were taken from me. I'm so glad you've come here today.

"And you, my dear Aunt Margaret, how can I ever thank you for all you did for me. When you heard that I was the sole-survivor of that awful crash, you came and took me home with you. You became my loving Auntie but mostly my mother. Thank you for bringing me up and giving such a good life. Mother and Father, know that I loved her and missed her as much as I love you and missed you."

The tall elegant man she knowns as her Father, James Anderson, steps forward and says, "We love you, too, Liz. Now we will speak with your familiar, Kip. Thank you for bringing her to be with us today, Kip. We congratulate your ability to control her thoughts. Was there much resistance to come today? She was so upset when Peter was called home two years ago. That was the reason the Universal Council sent you to her. She a settling influence, so that she would know her own mind on that Summer Solstice. Do you feel she is ready to be freed to continue her life journey on her own?"

*Liz is a strong entity and the Universal Council has underestimated her. She was the entity who brought the living Parallel Lives of Elizabeth together. She is the one who adjoined the dining tables so each dimension would be fused at the point of the golden stone in the floor, the same golden agate you placed in the cement floor of your cabin, many years ago. Today I will leave Liz. Rudy Sloan has come to her and they love each other. They should continue their lives together. Liz will not leave with you on this day. She will not give up a life with Rudy Sloan without a fight. Are you going to insist she return to U-ron-i-sis?*

"Don't say anymore, Kip. Let me talk to this daughter myself. She was born Elizabeth Ann Anderson. At the time of the accident this entity left to live her life with her Aunt Margaret who began calling her Liz. After graduating from the University, she married Peter Day. Do you agree with what I have said, Liz?

Looking at the entity known as James Anderson, Liz nods and says,

"Yes, Father, I understand everything you said and I agree that you said it correctly."

"Good, Now both of you must understand, if Liz refuses to return to U-ron-i-sis with us, the entity known as Zar must exit this dog's body and leave the animal with Liz. Liz will live out her life on Redcliff's Beach with no memory of what she experienced with you, Zar. You are to go to another planet beyond the galaxy Ellorentica to assist another entity. Are you willing to do this?"

*Totally, James. Does Jill agree to leave this Elizabeth to live out her life with this dog called Kip? If so, will you come back to receive her when her life has ended? What do you say, Jill?*

"Of course, Zar. Just as all parents have done since the beginning of time. Lives are as precious to us on U-ron-i-sis as anywhere else in the Universal Expanse. I nursed that child and loved her every moment of my life here on Earth. Whatever will make her happy, will make both her father and I happy. Did you know Rudy Sloan petitioned the Universal Council to let him step away from being an eternal caregiver to become a true human for the rest of his life in this dimension? Rudy Sloan says her loves Liz and her dog, Kip, and wants to be with them for the rest of this lifetime."

*Yes. He told me he would ask permission to stay on Earth and take her for his own. He loves the dog called Kip and will be a good husband and master of the dog. How do you respond, Rudy Sloan? Step forward now and speak for yourself.*

Immediately, Liz feels a movement beside her. When the entities known as James and Jill Anderson and Margaret step forward, the shake the hand of the man standing at Liz's side. After greeting the visitors, Rudy Sloan takes hold of Liz's hand and squeezes it gently. Turning her head, Liz smiles and says, "Hello darling Rudy. I'm so glad you're here. I was afraid you decided not to come today. I'd like you to meet my parents, James and Jill Anderson and my Aunt Margaret. Everyone, this is Rudy Sloan. He is my next door neighbor. He is the man I love and want to marry. We plan to live together for the rest of our lifetimes.

Will you give us your blessing before you return to U-ron-i-sis, Father? Mother? Aunt Margaret?"

"Yes, Liz. Rudy, we give our blessings and are happy for you both. We feel you have made a wonderful choice. We have known Rudy Sloan during several of our lifetimes. We have also Zar, the amazing entity that was the familiar within the dog you know as Kip. Zar is needed elsewhere in the Universe and will leave with us. Zar has said you no longer need his input. We know Rudy as a being of good character. We wish you both the best of lives. Go forth and live fully for all your lifetime. Jill and I proudly give our blessing to your future plans. Don't we, Jill?"

"Yes, we do, Liz. As your mother, I am very happy that you found another to share what time you have on Earth. Know this, Rudy, that when you and Liz return to your houses on Redcliff's Beach, you will no longer remember any of what has happened here in the crystal room. Both Kip and Rudy will be, as they should be, a good dog and a good man who love you totally, Liz. The entity known as Zar will not go with you. As I said, this entity is needed elsewhere. Is there anything that you wish to say to Liz before she leaves us, Margaret?"

"Yes, I want you to know you two have my best wishes for your new life. You were the best thing to happen to me, Liz. I will return to U-ron-i-sis for now and return only when it is time for you to join us on U-ron-o-sis. Goodbye, my darling child, I will see you when you come through to the shimmering shroud to the other side."

With this said, Margaret steps behind the others. James steps up to Kip and says, "Zar? Release yourself from Kip and stand beside Margaret. Please. Sir? Do it now."

At once, a bright glowing form flows from Kip's forehead and the animal whines loudly. As the image releases from the dog, it takes the shape of a small child who goes to Margaret and takes hold of one of her hands. Smiling at the entity, James says, "Thank you, Zar. You did that very nicely. Now it is time for you and Margaret to go to the Universal Council, as both of your next placements are ready to receive you."

Turing back Liz and Rudy, James says, "Please, hold each other's hands. The Universal Council insists that the decision you two have chosen be made permanent without outside interference. My darling daughter, Elizabeth Ann, it is time to let you go back to your life at Redcliff's Beach with Rudy Sloan and your dog Kip. I give you to each other for as long as you both shall live. Love each other totally for the rest of this lifetime and be happy. Once you are within your own dimension, what has happened in this crystal room will be wiped from your memories. From that moment on, Rudy, you are a human being who loves Liz Day and her dog named Kip."

Nodding at the elegant people before him, Rudy Sloan says, "I accept this change with pleasure. Liz Day is the only woman I have ever chosen. I will live my life as a true human-being and thank you and the Universal Council for fully understanding my request. May I take Liz and Kip home now?"

"Considered it is done." James says with a wave of his right hand.

When Liz awakens, she stretches her arms high over her head and sees she is on the chaise lounges on her beachside deck. "Mmmm, that little nap was just what I needed after that hike to the slap the touchstone. That mile seems to get longer each day I take it. Guess I'd better get inside and fix lunch. Are Rudy and Kip still out playing ball?"

Looking out over the sand dunes, her eyes catch sight of the man and dog splashing along the edge of the waves. The two are straight out from her cabin. However, today's tide has gone out far beyond where it had yesterday. Smiling contentedly, she watches their two shapes come and go within the mist rising off the sun heated beach and smiles as the man throws a ball and the dog runs after it, repeating the scene over and over.

"Oh, my man, I love him so…" Liz sings softly, knowing the man she loves, loves her and they both love and are loved by their dog. Swinging her legs off to one side of the chaise, Liz slips on her sandals and walks to the railing of the deck. For a long moment, she watches the two repeat their fetch and carry game. Then she cups her hands around her mouth and shouts, "Hey, you two, are you ready for lunch? How about a cold drink?"

Hearing her shout if not her words, both dog and man turn towards the house and the man raises his hands high over his head. Clapping his hands, he calls the dog which runs with the ball filling its mouth. Then both man and dog race across the hard packed sand, up the path through the sand dunes and take the steps up to the deck in one leap. When he reaches her, Rudy wraps his arms around Liz and sweeps her off her feet, swings her around twice, then kisses her mouth with the full passion of a new groom to his new bride.

While this is done, their dog named Kip simply drops a red ball at their feet and trots over to its water dish to lap fresh cold water. All is normal and good at the home of the Sloan family, Rudy, Liz and their dog, Kip.

No thoughts are exchanged by either ever again. Nor, if they were, would any or the three understand where they came from or what that meant.

# FIFTEEN

*June 20<sup>th</sup>—The Summer Solstice*
   *Beth*

**BETH** reaches the huge granite slab at the base of the north cliffs and crosses it quickly to stand in front of the large golden stone in the cliff face. Looking to her right, she sees Dandelion crouched nearby staring up at the ledges where hundreds of shore birds are stirring off their aeries. Laughing, Beth says, "its okay, girl. Don't you know by now that those birds are more afraid of you than you are of them? Come here, I'm not going to slap the touchstone until you are right next to me. You don't want to be left behind, do you? It's the Summer Solstice, remember? It's to be our biggest day ever."

As the cat creeps over to settle at her feet, Beth raises her right hand and shouts, "I declare this run good and done." As she slaps the golden stone, there is a loud cracking noise and both Beth and Dandy look up to see what caused the noise. In that second, both Beth and Dandy are flattened by the huge hunk of granite that has broken off the cliff face then falls exactly on the spot they are standing. Neither woman nor cat make a sound before being killed by this new slab of rock.

Beth tries to take in a breath that doesn't come for a split second she is overcome by panic. Then, Dandelion says,

*Do not be afraid, dear one. I am with you. Our two beings are no more. We are beyond fear, beyond pain and beyond caring. We soon meet and join with your parents, James and Jill Anderson. They are to escort us to the far side of the Universe, through the shimmering void you saw last week. Once there, you will meet with the Universal Council to hear where you are to go next. As you have lived out your highest self this next step will be your choice and that will happen when you are ready. At that time, I will also be told where I am needed and leave you to go wherever the Council intends me to help another.*

Immediately, Beth's essence moves to the side of the huge striped cat and sees they are floating above the fire-opal tiles within the crystal room. In front of the crystal thrones stand shimmering forms of similar beings. Knowing they are not who she is looking for, she whispers. "Dandy, where are the others? Where are Liz and Ann? Why do I feel so different? Did I shout my mantra or slap the touchstone wrong? Who are those beings by the thrones? Do you know who they are? Are you sure we are in the correct crystal room?"

*Yes, dear one, we are in the only crystal room and those entities in front of us are your parents, James and Jill Anderson. The other beings are there to assist us through the wormhole to the other side of the Universe. Remember the golden void at the edge of the Universe? We will now go through it to stand before the Universal Council. They will greet you and ask you your plans for eternity as you have reached the end of your lives on Earth. Do not be afraid, I will be with you until that decision is made by you.*

Right after the cat tells her this, the two taller beings step away from the others by the thrones and come to stand below Beth and Dandelion. The man raises one hand up to her and Beth takes it with both of her hands. As he pulls her down to him, the man says, "Elizabeth Ann, darling daughter, it is so good to see you again. We are James and Jill Anderson, your parents. We are here to take you with us now that you are done here on Earth. Your cat, Dandelion, will lead you through the shimmering void to the Universal Council. There your essence will hear what is planned for your next life. Do you have any questions?"

"Where are the other Elizabeth Anns? Why aren't Liz and Ann here? My Parallel Lives named Liz Day and Ann Anderson? We were told that we should come before dawn so we would be together and then meet with both you and Jill. Tell me, I demand to know, why aren't they here with me/"

As soon as she says this, the entity named Jill Anderson steps past her husband and pulls Beth down into her arms. Holding the essence known as Beth, Jill says. "Oh my darling daughter, my dear Elizabeth Ann, you no longer need your earthly body. You have reached the end of you last life on Earth. That life is gone forever. It was crushed by a giant slab of the cliff face after you slapped the touchstone and shouted your mantra. That dark shadow you saw, after you heard the stone split from the granite cliffs was that piece which broke off and fell onto the place where you and Dandelion were standing. As I said, your earthly body died instantly and your essence came into the crystal room to find us.

"Your others, Liz Day and Ann Anderson, as you have known them, are alive and well. They will continue to live until their earthly bodies fail, years from now. That is why they will not adjoin you today. James and I have met with Liz earlier and she chose to continue living her life with the man known as Rudy Sloan and her dog named Kip. The entity, called Zar, has left Kip and he is now a true dog, in all ways. Neither Liz nor Rudy will remember their time in the crystal room with us or with you or Ann. Ann is late and will miss us here in the crystal room. This being late is Ann's worst habit."

"These two Elizabeth Anns knew you as their original child, but there are others who are also from your essence and are here to adjoin with you." James tells Beth as he takes her hand with his. When Beth resists moving with him, James whispers, "Elizabeth Ann, I told you that you have others wanting to adjoin with you before we return to U-ron-i-sis by way of the wormhole."

This time, Beth's essence relaxes and floats above the tall man as he crosses the fire-opal tiles to the shimmering images standing in front of the crystal thrones. "Who are these others you talk about? I didn't know others would be joining with me. Why would they want to come with me?"

Stopping in front of the first essence, James tells Beth, "This is Eliza Staples. You do remember her, don't you? She was the Elizabeth Ann Anderson who was killed by your sister, Dee, last year when she went into your dimension by mistake. Please, take Eliza's hands and bring her to you and adjoin her to your essence."

"Nooo, no, no, no… I want Liz and Ann. I want my friends with me. Please, let me go back home. Give me back my darling orange cat, Dandelion. Dandy where are you? I'm not ready to leave my life. Please?"

*Stop this, Beth. You knew something wondrous was to happen today. You that was why I showed you the edge of the Universe. I told you it was to happen. Did you think it was a bedtime story? Now do as James has asked you to do. Take Eliza's hands and bring her into your essence. Eliza didn't want to leave her life when she was killed by your sister, Dee McGowan. Simply step up to her essence as touch noses. Then you'll see how easy it is to adjoin her essence to yours.*

As Dandelion says this, Eliza's essence floats to Beth's essence and says, "Darling Beth, I returned so we could adjoin and travel to the Universe Council as one."

"Well done, my child." Jill Anderson and hugs Elizabeth Ann as soon as the two entities become one. "Now meet Bette Gardner, the mother of the young man you knew as Neil Gardner. Take her hands and pull her into you as you did Eliza. Wonderful. The next Elizabeth Ann is actually three of your Parallel Lives who left their dimensions to be adjoined with your essence. There, it is done. Now, you are completed as our child, Elizabeth Ann. You have adjoined with all but the last two, Ann and Liz. They have chosen to live out their lives in their present dimensions. As I tell you this, they have forgotten you existed and have no memory of your ever being part of their lives. We will leave the crystal cave by way of the wormhole and go first to U-ron-i-sis. Then, your animal familiar, Dandelion, will lead you to and through the shimmering void he took you to see last week. Though there, you will meet with the Universal Council awaits to hear where you wish to exist for all eternity."

James Anderson moves to Jill's side and says, "Dear One, it is time for us to take our child and leave. Dandelion, please lead us into the wormhole and back to U-ron-i-sis and out to where the Universal Council awaits. Beth, please follow Dandy into the wormhole. You may take hold of your mother's hand or ride on the back of the great bold beast you call Dandelion, if it gives you comfort."

As the essence of the original child named Elizabeth Ann Anderson grabs onto the thick fur of the large Tiger and sits upon his back, she says, "Stay with me, Dandelion. I don't want to be separated from you."

# SIXTEEN

*June 20<sup>th</sup>—The Summer Solstice*
*Ann*

**ANN** and Honey reach the top of the north cliffs just as the sun breaks over the mountain tops, run past the stonewall and cliff top kitchen and take the path straight up the steep slope of the high berm that hides the opening into the crystal room. Suddenly, a brilliant beam of light shoots into the sky from the center of the berm and the glare blinds Ann.

Covering her eyes with one arm, she stops and shouts, "What is that? Not yet, wait for me, wait for me. Liz, Beth, wait for me, I'm coming. I'll be there in a minute. Wait for me. Beth, Liz, wait for me. I'll be with you in seconds. I'm here. I'm coming for our Summer Solstice."

As if an answer to her words, a rush of air roars up from the cave's opening, sending rock, dirt and vegetation high into the sky. Simultaneously, with that massive upchuck of debris, the ground shakes violently under Ann's feet and causes her to stumble. Losing her balance, she falls backward and hits the ground with a pounding thud which knocks her unconscious. Immediately, her limp body bounces off the path and tumbles down the steep slope towards the cliff top kitchen. In the next few seconds, her body slams into the end of the stonewall she built years before. When her ribs whack the end of the wall, the structure slowly tumbles into a long row of stones in place of the wall.

Her unconscious body lays motionless next to this pile of stones and Ann does not hear the roaring eruption that continues as the steep berm collapses inward. Then there is another quaking rumble as the cave erupts, heaving tons of debris several hundreds of feet into the sky. Surge after surge of powerful explosions hurl massive boulders and debris high above the cliff top's opening. When the debris reaches its apex, there is a second of silence as those rocks, sand and plant life hang suspended high in the air.

Then, in the time it takes to blink an eye, all this debris drops back into the enormous hole left by the huge eruptions with a roaring crash. At that time, this massive amount of debris fills the vast void and all those pieces settle together with one fierce earthshaking thud.

When the dust settles over the cliff tops, there is only silence. Not one seabird cries as tall clumps of seagrass fall into place around groupings of boulders which now cover the nearly flat surface across the cliff top. Then, as if to put an exclamation point at the end of a dramatic sentence, one lone boulder lands and rolls slowly to stop next to Ann's right foot.

As the stone adjusts to its new location, Ann begins to stir and her right leg nudges the large boulder. Opening her eyes, she pushes herself into a sitting position and leans against this same boulder. Looking around at the cliff tops, she sees Honey sitting beside a shiny black enameled steel bench. Next to this bench is a wide path of crushed rock and she assumes this is where she had been running when she tripped and fell.

"Honey? What the hell did I trip on? Ouch, my elbows and knees are a scraped mess. Well, I don't think I broke any bones. But, damn, these scrapes sure sting."

Reaching over to the metal bench, Ann uses its arm to pull herself up. Moving over to it, she feels each part of her body to see if anything else is damaged. Glad to see there are only the scrapes and some bruises, she sits on the seat of the metal bench and moves each leg and arm in a circle. Then, she bends forward to stretch her back muscles and twists to the left and right. Though she feels a bit of soreness, nothing makes her scream with agony and Ann sighs loudly, leans back against the hard cold metal back of the bench and watches the sunrise over the Cascade Mountain Range.

Looking to the south, she sees lights on in her cabin and she says to Honey, "Look how cozy our home looks from up here. Dad certainly knew what he was doing when he built it on that high basalt point. Hey, now I remember why I tripped over my feet. I glanced down at the beach and caught my toe on something at the edge of the path. Luckily, I fell to the right or the path and not to the left. I could have rolled off the edge. Guess Dana is right. It is too dark to run before sunrise. I'll slow down and walk until sunrise. I love to get up here before the crowds do."

Listening to the waves crash against the cliff face far below. Ann stares down the bench and sees more lights flicker on in the many homes strewn along Shoreline Drive. Six miles to the south, rows of street lights twinkle showing the area of the village that wraps around the resorts at that end of Redcliff's Beach.

Sighing loudly, Ann says, "Look down to the south, Honey. Only our cabin and acreage is unchanged. All the rest of the beach is filling up with new homes and motels. I'm very certain that our folks are pleased that Dana and I have kept the land and cabin the same as they left it to us years ago."

Thinking about her family, Ann stares at the high deep sand dunes which cover her beach. Suddenly a loud bit of jazz fills the air and her jacket pocket vibrates. Pulling her phone from the pocket, she says, "Hey Dana, I was just thinking of you. You're going to love what I did when I was near the first metal bench on the cliff tops. Yes, I did. I tripped and fell. How did you know that? You saw me do it? With Dad's binoculars? You knew it was me? Okay, tell Cliff if he stops laughing, I'll make him blue berry waffles when I get back. Dinner at your place? Sure. Okay, five it is. See you then. Love ya both, bye."

Returning the phone to her jacket pocket, Ann stands and says,

"Honey, we came up to walk out to the point so let's get going. Where's your lead? Good, it's still on you collar. Okay? Let's go, girl."

As they move along the wide path that follows the edge of the cliffs, they waken hundreds of seagulls and terns which rise off their aeries along the ledges. The flocks of birds scream their intention before soaring out toward the western horizon. Smiling as the raucous birds fly away from the cliffs, Ann says, "Honey, isn't it wonderful to live at Redcliff's Beach and come each morning to Dad's State Park. He worked long hours and still had time to work with the State and community to keep these cliffs a park for public use. He lived for five years afterwards and was proud how the park was named in his honor, The James Anderson State Park. Now everyone coming up here can enjoy the view over Redcliff's Beach and those beaches to the north."

With Honey trotting ahead of her, Ann follows the winding path as it moves through the mounds of boulders piled within the thick stands of seagrass which cover the nearly flat cliff tops. When a large ground squirrel pokes its head from between two of the rocks and chuckles at the, Honey pulls the lead out of Ann's hand and runs after it. Laughing, Ann gives the dog a moment or two to stick her nose between the piles of boulders and woof softly.

Then she steps off the path and catches hold of the dog's lead as she says, "No, no, girl, you're not supposed to chase the fauna into the flora in any of the State Park. Especially not the one your Grandpa created. You can only sniff the breezes and point at whatever lives up here."

As the trail rounds the last large boulder, it widens into a viewpoint with five black enameled steel benches facing the cliff edge. Sitting on the last one, Ann looks out to the western horizon and sees the sunrise's colors are edging the sweeping waves a bright pink.

Looking down below the cliffs, she exclaims, "Honey, look below us. The tide is out way beyond the normal low. Oh, of course, it's the Summer Solstice. The tides are going to be the highest and lowest of the year. Gosh, Honey, when we head back home, we'll go down on those tide flats and I'll let you off lead. You and I'll get to have a good run along the waves."

Enjoying the view from this most western point on the north cliffs on Redcliff's Beach, Ann combs her fingers through the soft golden fur on the dog and Honey heaves a big sigh. When the large dog lays her head on Ann's knee, she says, "Thanks for being my friend, Honey. I love you so much. I could probably stay here all day, but it looks as if other people have the same idea we did and are coming up to see the sunrise. Let's go back down the trail and run out to the edge of the waves."

As the two follow the wide circling path, through the grouping of boulders and seagrasses, they make their way along the north side of the cliffs. Finally the path winds back to the entrance of the park and Ann and Honey reach the last grouping of the huge boulders and tall grasses covering the center of the cliff top. There are no thoughts of the once high berm up from the cliff top kitchen. Nor is there any thoughts of the opening that took them into a large cave room filled with crystals and fire-opal tiles. Nor is there any memories of Ann talking to Honey and hearing the dog's answers.

Ann and Honey are happy and contented in this new dimension brought about from the massive eruptions which obliterated the cliff tops and crystal room. The eruptions were brought about by the Universal Counsel so Ann and Honey would never remember the dimension where they lived knowing the Parallel Lives of Elizabeth Ann Anderson and their animal familiars. The Universal Council made certain the shift of Ann's dimension would settle into an orbital plain around the planet known as Earth, far from where they'd known their others.

The new dimension holds firmly within Earth's rotations and Ann only knows what she sees and her memories are only those which the Universal Counsel provided for her. Thus, all is good and true, making certain Ann will live out her lifetime as any normal human being would.

As the two beings follow the crushed rock path towards the east, they stop to chat with others who have come to the cliff tops to enjoy the view of the wild beaches to the north and watch the sunrise colors now brilliantly coloring the sky.

As they walk past the metal bench she had fallen beside, the exact spot where her stonewall and driftwood kitchen had once been, Ann has no memory of the differences from what she sees at that moment. It's only when she gets to where the path ends at the edge of the beach that a puzzled look crosses Ann's face and she turns to look up at the State Park for a split second. Then, giving her head a slight shake, she quickly dislodges the unknown shadow from her mind.

Seeing the dog's happy anticipation, Ann unclips the dog's lead and as the golden animal runs into the waves, she follows. Then both run south towards the copper roofed cabin sitting exactly where James Anderson built it for his family.

## *The End*

CPSIA information can be obtained
at www.ICGtesting.com
Printed in the USA
FSOW01n1735270517
34712FS